I0831937

Ways

of

Love

Publisher's Cataloging-in-Publication data
Names: White, Franklin, author.
Title: Ways of love / Franklin White.
Description: Atlanta, GA: Blue/Black Press, 2022.
Identifiers: ISBN: 978-0-9789990-1-8
Subjects: LCSH Family--Fiction. | Relationships--Fiction. | African American trade--Fiction. | Atlanta (Ga.)--Fiction. | BISAC FICTION / General Classification: LCC PS3623.H5749 W39 2022 | DDC 813.6- dc23
ISBN -978-0-9789990-6-3

Ways of Love

Franklin White

Blue

Also by Franklin White

Fed Up with the Fanny

Cup of Love

Til' Death Do Us Part (Short Stories)

Team Mom

Money For Good

More Money For Good

First Round Lottery Pick

Potentially Yours

Joy and Pain

"Bet you didn't know -I was coming with a smack."

- Larenz

Wine

The beginning of her night is like a movie, a blockbuster, in fact. Ania Ways is blissful and has just dropped her robe on the floor; she's feeling no pain, listening to music, swaying back and forth on her second glass of a 1988 Masseto Toscana IGT from Tuscany, Italy. This is the same bottle of merlot she promised her husband, Larenz, she wouldn't open without him, but hey, things change; the loving couple will just have to buy another. This moment is long overdue for Ania since Tuesday after a client she's been consulting on a fashion photo portfolio for their magazine had the gall to turn it into a filthy nudity spread. The said company thought it would be a good idea to falsely mention her as creative director with her name on a social media-made video sprawled in the credits which is so far from the truth. It takes her the rest of the week to get it straightened out because her name is her brand, and there is no way she is going out like that. So, now after her workflow drama, she is in dire need of one of those old-school Calgon moments she witnessed her grandmother have in her small, two-bedroom house when she was a little girl, and then too her mother, in their two-bedroom house on the south-side of Chicago. But there will not be any soaking tonight: Ania defers for steam in her recently renovated bathroom shower, complete with an Exira thermostatic system where the water is getting ready to touch her body in every direction in her artistic vintage fifty-year-old home in Atlanta's Cascade Heights. At the same time, she listens to Jill Scott belt out "A Long Walk" through the magical surround sound system and it sets her mood perfectly. Ania loves the song so much she surrenders to the songstress from Philly and her phenomenal voice as it soothes her soul; then when she steps inside the shower she begins to sing along with Jill as though she helped write the Grammy nominated hit and the words are subliminally appearing like a karaoke machine right in front of her eyes. While the water splashes her body and Ania sings along with Jill, they sing the part about their men not being squeaky clean and surprisingly and very much wanted; her man, Larenz Ways, rolls back the shower doors and steps his naked body inside with his queen. Ania is pleasantly surprised. She smiles then takes his phone out of his hand, places it on the shower ledge next to hers then hands Larenz her glass of wine. He takes a sip and instantly notices it's the special bottle they have been saving then places the glass back down and wraps his arms around her body right after Ania places her finger on his lips to silence him from mentioning the wine. What a wonderful end to a crazy week, the mood is set, Ania is pleased and Larenz is most definitely showing Ania how much he appreciates her by giving and accepting her love. They are a beautiful site of coco love and the colors of their bodies are complimentary and a similar picture should be painted and placed on the mantel of bedrooms to remind couples of a relationship that can flourish and feed their spirit. Larenz is so into the moment as he kisses Ania all over her body. He kneels in front of her, and as soon as his tongue touches her stomach, it's as though Jill's words to her hit song freeze in place along with the music when the phone rings. Larenz stops giving her the ultimate pleasure, swipes water from his face to answer the phone while Ania exhales with disappointment and much frustration. With a very high pitch tone she says, "Are you serious—right now?"

He says, "Hold on baby, hold on a sec." Larenz wipes off the mist and steam on his phone and realizes the call is from his business partner, JT; he sighs at the interruption, but with so much going on, it's a must take call. Ania picks up her wine, gulps it down attempting to wash away her setback she hopes to put back in motion in the next couple of seconds. Larenz swipes the water from his face again. "Yeah, hello?"

His business partner doesn't waste time. JT says, "Hey man, where you at? I'm going into the club now."

Larenz looks at Ania as she puts her wine back down and starts kissing and biting on his neck. Larenz kisses her on her shoulder and she is making it very hard for Larenz to focus. JT detects the faint sound of the shower in the background. Larenz struggles to say, "I'm someplace special. Somewhere you could never be my brother, believe that. JT what do you want?"

"Well, you need to dry off and get down here for this meeting. We have numbers to crunch."

"Meeting? Numbers? What're you talking about JT?" Larenz tries to resist the feel of Ania's French manicured nails running down his neck and slowly going down the front of his body.

"I told you L, I'd be at the club at eight. You know– about the commercial property. Larenz the property is getting too expensive man, we need to look over the books and chat about getting spending under control."

Ania is very close to her favorite spot on Larenz and is enjoying watching him struggle with the feelings she is shooting through his body while he talks.

Larenz says, "Look JT can't this wait until tomorrow?"

"Hell no, checks need to be signed and handed out to contractors, first thing in the morning. But first, you need to look over the books and sit down and chat make sure game is tight."

Ania looks up at Larenz and he smiles at her. But she is starting to lose all hope.

Larenz says, "Look bruh, you're making this very hard right now. I'm in the middle of something."

"No, that's your lovely doing that." JT laughs at his own joke. "Hate to do it to you but you gotta' take a rain check and handle this business. You hate surprises and I sure as hell do, so let's get down to business to make sure these numbers are good."

Larenz groans, he looks at Ania and pauses. She picks up on the hesitation, takes a deep breath, yanks his stiffness and comes close to making Larenz buckle while he tries to mask the shock of the pain she causes so JT won't overhear him. Ania exhales, snatches her towel and leaves the shower. Larenz keeps his eyes on her body as she exits and shakes his head in disappointment mixed with his pain. "Damn it, JT, give me about twenty minutes."

JT tells him, "I'll be at the bar with a drink." Then he waves at a few ladies on their way inside of Larenz's establishment, Club Nickels.

"You better pay for it too," Larenz shoots back before he disconnects.

Larenz doesn't have to receive a memo stating he has just messed all the way up. It wasn't as bad as last month when he promised Ania he was going to come home and work her body until she begged him to stop because this time things weren't planned. He actually just came home to get some invoices he left in his home office and the situation presented itself so, in his mind Ania would be able to understand. Larenz steps out the shower dripping wet and looks around for Ania, and when he finds her, she has dried herself off and is sliding into the thong she specifically purchased for Larenz to focus his eyes on, then she quickly starts to apply some shea all over her body with plenty of pent-up sexual attitude.

"Here, baby– let me help you with that," Larenz suggests.

"Don't do me L. You know you need to put on some clothes and run down to the club. Don't even try it." Ania puts more shea in the palm of her hand and is applying it with the quickness on her feet.

"I wouldn't do you baby, not my style."

"That's the problem. You didn't."

"But I will. I promise you."

"But you didn't, and the time was just right."

"Yeah, it was a special moment. But can I be honest with you while I'm standing here butt-ass naked? Can I do that please?"

She smiles a bit because he has always been kind of goofy and she loves it. "What is it Larenz?"

"Why are you drinkin' the good wine? That was for us."

Sarcastically with a twist of love she says, "It was for us. Didn't you get some?"

"What, it was a lil' ass taste? It was supposed to be for a special moment."

"It was close to being special, Larenz."

"But you didn't know I was coming home?"

"Yes, I did, I had a feeling," She smiles.

"Right." He walks over closer to her.

"Look, I'm sorry it seems like it just never stops. Always something."

"You're right always something, besides me."

"C'mon, that's not fair. It's just a quick meeting with JT at the club, then I'll be right back."

"Yeah, right."

"Look, c'mon go with. After I'm done with JT we'll have a few drinks then come back here and get things poppin' again."

Ania shakes her head no. "Un, unh, I'm good. It's going to be hard recapturing our beautiful, spontaneous much needed moment. It was perfect. So, natural and unexpected, just perfect." There's a knock at the door and Larenz keeps his eyes on Ania because she is already on her way to answer it. "Plus, that's my girl Jill at the door," she hollers back at him.

"Jill? Oh, I see, I see. You were going to play me for a quickie. Is that what we're doing?"

She turns around and smiles. "Hey, it is-what it is. I'll take whatever I can get, whenever I can get it at this point."

Larenz just stands looking around for his clothes, so he can go meet with JT, as he can hear the ladies start to chat it up right after Ania opens the door.

"Hey, girl." Jill says. "Look at you just glowing. What have you been doing?"

"Nothing, trust me it's just the shea."

"Oh, just the shea–I hear you, Ms. Lady."

"Umm…hmm."

Jill looks around. "Where's that crazy husband of yours? I see the freshly washed 740 out there. He's the reason for the disappointment I hope?"

"He's in here someplace, c'mon you gotta' try some of this wine."

"I sure do." Jill raises her voice a few octaves. "Hey, Larenz guess who's here and about to drink up all your fine wine?"

The ladies start to laugh. Ania adds, "Yup, gonna' drink it all up baby!"

The Nerve

It takes Larenz a few minutes more than he anticipates to get down to the club to meet with JT because he wants to get the ladies honest opinion on the merlot they are drinking up since it was supposed to be saved for a special occasion and he isn't able to sit back and enjoy it with them. Then the Atlanta traffic is mad crazy on this Friday night even though they only live six miles from the club. When Larenz arrives at Club Nickels, as usual there is a nice crowd flowing through having dinner and drinks. Even a poet walks up on stage and performs an expressive set that is moving and full of emotion. The guests cheer and shout for more which brings joy to Larenz's heart because it's why he opened this joint. As soon as he moved to Atlanta so many years ago he felt the city needed a place of expression, and he has proudly filled the void. JT is at the bar, and when Larenz sees him, Larenz pats him on the back; they go into the office to chop it up, and it only takes them a few minutes to get into the topic of discussion.

Larenz is stunned to say the least. "Man, where is all this coming from? When we started, we had the budget and the plan and now, it's like we never even went over any of this?" Larenz looks down at his drink sitting on his desk, and he wants another, so he reaches in the drawer, pulls out a bottle of Hennessy, pours another then slides the bottle over to JT.

JT gets a glass, sets it so close it clinks, then he moves the glass a bit and says, "Well my brother, this is the challenge of commercial real estate. You find dead beat things along the way; every floor and room can't be perfect, so you either patch them up or pass them along, and hope nothing bad happens."

Larenz looks at him intensely. "Like the building down in Florida? We are definitely not trying to have anything remotely similar attached to our name—that was such a sad day bruh."

"Exactly, GOD rest their souls." Larenz and JT raise their glasses to the fallen and sip.

"So, what's the plan?" Larenz wants to know. He always listens heavily to JT's advice. They have known one another since Larenz and Ania moved to Atlanta from Chicago. JT has witnessed Larenz's growth and vise-versa their partnership has been a ride, and they are doing very well for themselves. JT basically works as the business manager and self-proclaimed personal security for Larenz because he is so damn big, while Larenz uses his creative side for ideas. First, it was the club Larenz wanted to start and call it Club Nickels because he didn't have two to rub together for a club when he started out over twenty years ago and didn't know how getting the club up and going was ever going to happen. But he would always listen to JT at the barber shop, talking all his knowledge about black business when he had hair and now that he doesn't the advice he was kicking about investments, real estate, and (401)k's is turning out to be true because the brothers are getting paid in all areas. "I really don't want to put any more money in the building, JT." Larenz tells him.

JT sits up closer to the desk. "Look, it's not exactly, an all-hands-on deck emergency. It's just a warning sign that we have to watch every penny on this deal."

Larenz is taken back a bit. "Hold up, did you say this isn't an emergency?"

"No, nah, we're going to be good." JT leans back into his chair then takes a sip.

"You sure acted like this here was an emergency?"

JT smiles. "It's my job."

"I should throw this glass and pop your ass across your forehead with it. Burning up, what I had going on."

"Don't worry brother. You're still the man."

Larenz takes another drink and says, "You ain't never lied."

"And we know as men, if it's yours, it will be there when you get back."

Larenz thinks about his words. "Now this is true, my brother, this is true."

Then there is a knock at the door. JT gets up answers, and their visitor pops his head in, showing only his face and his shining hair that one might think he is still sparsely blasting a few pumps of activator on the top; at least using some afro-sheen mixed with Royal Crown pomade. His fake smile is manufactured like someone just told him he was the man or he has heard it so much, he really believes it himself. He says, "Well, well, well, I have been through Atlanta frontward, backward, sidewards several times and have never ever got my invite to this wonderful landmark, so, I took it upon myself to stop by this joint." Then he does the smile thing again. "Mos def-it's been a long time." For a minute Larenz can't believe his eyes let alone the balls this guy has by showing up in his place. Larenz left this bad news negro in Chicago and has forgotten all about him.

The visitor wiggles his way into the office and finally closes his mouth as he looks around and is almost way too hyped for the moment and shrugs and adjusts his shoulders as though he is relieved to make it inside. "Man, it's been a minute. When we were younger, and they told us time flies, we never wanted to hear it, but look at us now, grown ass men up in here, who have made big moves." He reaches out his hand towards JT. "How you doing– Bill Cash." Right away JT knows this guy isn't from The A; his drip was much too over the top and even had the first two buttons on his shirt unbuttoned, looking like one of the old school Bee Gees or, better yet, a Miami Vice detective. JT looks over at Larenz trying to get a read on him, right before he continues to try to take over the room with his intro. "Me and this guy sitting behind the desk go way back."

JT says, "Nice to meet you."

Bill's eyes travel back to Larenz. "What's going on Larenz, how you making it my brother?"

Larenz has already gotten over the surprise of seeing this dirt bag in his place of business and it takes no time to reach into his memory bank and pull out some of the Chicago ready to throw hands mode. "What can I do for you Bill? And who let you back here?"

Bill picks up on the attitude; he's from Chi-town too but he goes shade mode. "Now L, you know how things are when you get some notoriety in the world, people tell you things and let you do even more." Bill looks around his office a bit then drags out his next statement like he is singing or something. "This is nice... I've heard a lot about Club Nickels. You got some poetry, some live music, stage performances….food, drinks, nice…very nice."

Larenz says, "Maybe you didn't hear me, what're you doin' here?"

"C'mon now, I'm just stopping by to check you out, say hello, whatnot."

"Without an invite?"

"C'mon bruh, we go way back. All the way back to the times when we didn't have nothing and didn't know how to get what we thought we wanted. But hey, look at us now. You have come to Atlanta done your thang and I know you've heard all, about me and what I got going on." Bill looks down at his own shoes and outfit enjoying the view of his ensemble.

JT glances over at Larenz.

"No, I haven't," Larenz says right before he nods to JT. "You ever heard about this guy JT?" JT shakes his head no then starts looking where he was going to grab this fool who is interrupting their meeting because he was in tune with the attitude Larenz is giving this Cash guy and is at the ready to pop.

"Yeah, right L," Bill brushes off.

Larenz says, "Okay, you came in here, to tell me what—it's good to see you or some shit? Why the visit?"

Bill says, "Proposition, my brother."

"Proposition?"

Bill gives a look at JT.

Larenz says, "He's good. Matter of fact you can't even talk to me if he's not around."

"Oh, it's like that?"

JT tells him, "No other way—believe it."

"Okay then. Look here gentlemen, I've been thinking L during my flight on my private jet from Cali with my new group. You know it would be a hell of a thing if I can showcase my up-and-coming investment in your fine establishment for a few weeks?"

Larenz doesn't even give it any thought and places his hand down on his desk like Judge Ito tapping down his gavel back in the day in the Simpson trial. "Nah, we good."

Bill laughs, "Wait a minute now, hear me out. Can you just do that? Everyone knows, if you get the buzz in The A you can create buzz all across the world. Atlanta is definitely the place to set off a career. Don't you agree?"

"Yeah, I know because I played a part getting it this way. We get it poppin' it's not a secret. Am I right, JT?"

"It happens here for sure," JT lets him know.

Bill tries to reel them both in. "Exactly, so what I'm proposing is; I have this group I'm putting together. I mean they are so new I haven't even thought of a name yet. I'm leaning towards "Raw" because they are just that and you know how niggas always trying to go raw I think it would stick." JT can't believe this guy and squints his eyes trying to listen to this gibberish with his quick talking self.

"Are you serious?" Larenz wants to know. "Raw– because people like to go– raw? I should make you turn around and walk up out of here with that ignorant mess."

"Hella' serious, one thing about me my marketing is unquestionable. As I was saying these ladies have a nice lyrical side to them smooth, something your poetry fans can gravitate to, you know like Floetry use to do, back in the day. Soulful and raw, you'll love them."

Larenz looks at JT then back at Bill and says, "I love Floetry but I think I'm going to have to pass."

Bill smiles. "Thought you might be on that, but here's where it gets interesting for you. I'm willing to pay you, to let them rock out here for a few weeks and I will give you the entire gate at the door because this is how much I believe in these sisters, future."

Larenz and JT's eyes meet, JT coyly gives Larenz a look as though it's worth a thought. Larenz says, "So, you come up in here, offer to use my space at whatever cost I decide and give me one-hundred percent of the gate? So, what you making?"

"Look at me baby, does it look like I need some shit? Huh? I make stars and what I spend here with you, will be just a small price on what I make when we're done."

Larenz shakes his head in agreement but he's not impressed. "Nah, man, I'm good. But good luck."

Bill looks at Larenz and has a feeling his decision is deeper than he is leading on. "Okay, okay cool. I understand. Look, I'll be in town for a minute, so if you change your mind look a brother up." Bill wishes them a good night then reaches for the door then pauses. "Hey, I saw Ania, on the way in with one of her girls. Let her know, I said it was nice seeing her again." Bill opens the door and walks out and he can feel Larenz zeroing in on him as he walks out.

JT and Larenz have a slight look of disbelief. Maybe they both are thinking that this guy Bill had a lot of nerve walking into the establishment without an appointment and thinking someone would jump at an opportunity. Larenz might have listened more intently if it wasn't for Bills level of arrogance and egotism, he's been on since his days in Chicago. To top it off, he had Ania's name in his mouth which is definitely a no-no. Larenz turns around and pushes a button which allows him to see out on the club floor through a tinted window and Bill was right. Ania is at the bar drinking with Jill.

Club Night

After the ladies drank some of the high value wine back at the house Ania decides to call the clubs driver to come pick them up so they can continue to unwind and turn up even another notch. Their drinks are sent to their table on sight and they take in the atmosphere and happenings inside all the while Ania is in stitches listening to Jill and her antics.

"Really?" Ania wants to know. She can't believe the stories coming out of Jills mouth about a former lover of many years past.

"Gurl, yes and I mean every time too. He would put that thang exactly where I like it and keep it there until I …"

"Uh…uh no stop. Up in here in my man's establishment talking about some old-school dick."

"Well, I ain't lying I mean it would be a different thing altogether if I was lying but on my soul, the old-school dick is where it's at. He would just lay his thing up in my guts…."

"Wait, what, your guts?"

"Yes, girl, my guts. He was so far up in me I thought it was going to come out of my mouth. And it just sat there and I enjoyed it. I-am-not with what these young boys and all their smashing, grabbing, hitting nonsense they're out here talking about. Just put it in me and let me squeeze it, I'll be alright."

"See, you are just nasty."

"Yes indeed, yes I am– so toast to it."

They raise their glasses.

Ania switches it up. "So, how are things going with you and your man mentally?"

"We're good."

"Good to hear."

"I mean, if we can get from under the business of music and just be about the music together."

"What's going on?"

"Well, I want to sign a record deal, but Kerry wants to keep touring and doing our own thing without restrictions and the record company in our pocket."

"Can't you do both?"

"Nope, cause Viper records wants us both and if Kerry doesn't want to come on board then there is no deal."

"Wow."

"He says, it's all about the touring money. Doesn't want to give it up. We do pretty good on tour and the record company will want a piece if we sign with them and Kerry is not going for the stick-up."

Ania says, "Well, you know you're always welcome to come in here and do what you do until you decide. It's always packed when y'all are here. Just let me know and it's on."

"I really appreciate you friend. I really do."

"You're welcome."

The ladies take in the vibe for a moment while Kashif's hit, *Lover Turn Me On* is playing in the background setting the mood just fine.

"So, how are things on your end?" Jill wants to know.

"Busy as hell."

"Like that?"

"So, Larenz says, I can't seem to get a minute with this man."

"Well, he's been on the move, I can see with this club and all the real estate."

"I know, but can a girl get a vacation, some alone time? Can we enjoy the fruit of all this labor or something? This work, work, work, thing is getting tired."

Jill says, "You ain't never lied."

"Now don't get me wrong. I like my space and I'm not the clingy, baby, baby, what you doing type. But just that quality time is what I want more of, not trying to squeeze out a quickie every time I see you, 'cause it's been so long since we been together."

Jill smiles, "Wait a minute now, them quickies give you that big "O" from time to time, so don't go cancelling them out altogether."

"There you go, girl stop. But the good news is…."

Jill pushes, "Tell it, 'cause I love to hear it."

"Well, Nicole has done so well in therapy that her doctor is cool with her moving in with us and staying in the guest house and from there we can help her get back out here living her life, the way she deserves."

"Oh, my goodness. Now that is good news, I'm so proud of her. How long has it been?"

"Going on four years since they detected her problem and a little over two since she's been in rehab. I mean you should see her she's focused, happy just ready to get back to living as normal life as she can."

"This is wonderful. I only wish my sister peace and happiness in her new journey."

"Now, I don't know exactly when she's getting discharged, but after she's settled we're going to have a small intimate get together to welcome her home, right here."

"Say less, I wouldn't miss it for the world."

–

Larenz and JT chop it up for about an hour or so more before JT mentions he has a late dinner date and just as soon as he leaves the office, there is a knock at the door, and Larenz invites them in. He straightens his desk and grabs his suit jacket because he is ready to call it a night himself. "What's up Calvin?"

"What's good boss man? Just wanted you to know I just dropped Ania and her friend Jill off. I knew you were back here in a meeting with JT, so I didn't want to disturb you. But your queen is at home safe and sound."

"Thanks, I really appreciate that."

"No problem. Do you need a ride home?"

"Nah, I'm good."

"Okay, I'm going to go out here on the floor until they close up." Calvin takes a step towards the door and Larenz calls out to him. "Yeah, boss?"

"Dig, earlier tonight during my meeting with JT some cat from way back made his way to my office."

Calvin is surprised. "In here? I didn't see anyone come back here, could have been when I was parking the car after I picked up Ania from your place."

Larenz thinks on it. "Yeah, yeah, could be."

"Everything all right though?"

"Yeah, it's good. Just caught me off guard a bit."

"That's not good, boss man, I'll try to find out how he got back here and let you know."

"My man."

"Anything else?"

"No, that's it. How you doin' otherwise? You've been out here grinding hard Calvin don't think your hustle isn't unnoticed."

"Thanks, appreciate it."

"Everything good? I mean, how long have we known each other?"

"Ever since I was walking down the sidewalk in front of the club and you were getting boxes out your car and I asked you if you needed some help."

Larenz thinks on it. "Bruh, that seems like it was just yesterday."

"Sure does."

"We done made babies, raised them and still out here making things happen." Larenz catches the look on Calvin's face at the mention of his kid. "Yo, what's up with that look, everything good with the family?" Calvin hesitates. "What's up Calvin?"

"Just my son, this guy has me going thru it…"

"Cameron? He okay?"

"Yeah man, I mean he's a good kid and I know we all did questionable things coming up when we were trying to find our way, but some of the crap he's doing, going against family rules is not sitting right with me."

"Well, we family, talk to me."

Calvin takes a deep breath. It would be a welcomed relief to just get it off his mind so he flowed with the opportunity. "Okay, so he comes to me five, six months ago and told me he needed some money for something or another, thirty-five-hundred to be exact. I gave him the money on the strength that he would get it back to me before my anniversary since he has a job and he was going to pay me in installments. But hell, I ain't got one payment and my anniversary done rolled up on me and I can't do what I want to do with Kris and Cam's walking around acting like he doesn't owe me a thing. And now I find out his ass not even working; like he told me he was."

Larenz says, "Bruh the ones you love do it to you all the time don't they?"

"What it seems. We didn't do that to our parents though. GOD rest their souls."

"Not in our DNA. It's the way they living bruh, what they seeing out here, all this fake reality blinding their minds."

Calvin tightens his face and says, "And we left out here trying to make up for it 'cause we love our kids, don't want to see them without and they turn around and leave you ass out."

"Look man, don't sweat it. What were you going to do for your anniversary?"

Just the thought of it brings a smile to Calvin's face. "Bruh, was going to hit the Bahamas and relax. I mean we are over twenty in the game. I need to do something nice; it's not like I'm the easiest mufuka' to get along with. Kris put up over twenty with me, my own mama kicked me out at eighteen."

They both laugh. Larenz says, "Look here, you're going to the Bahamas bruh and celebrate this black love."

"How, as a stow away?"

"Nope, 'cause I'm going to make it happen. No worries."

"Say what?"

"Oh, yeah, you've been a part of this from the ground up. Take it as a gift from me and Ania."

"Boss man, I can't."

"You can and you will, I will have JT cut you a check so you can set it up." Calvin can't believe it and Larenz walks up to him and says, "Congratulations black man. Congrats to you and your queen, hey you never know, I might just go with Ania when you get back. Hell, I think I will. Now, go home and enjoy the rest of your night. We will get Cam straightened out it only takes time."

Calvin turns to open the door then turns around. "I really appreciate this."

"No problem, enjoy."

Late Convo

Ania is still up when Larenz walks through the door, close to eleven-thirty, because a late-night show is on, and the television screen is mute. Sade's "*Soldier of Love*" is playing softly all through the house. Larenz places his keys on the table, and Ania walks up to him gives him a glass of wine.

"Here baby, I saved you some of the wonderful merlot."

He smiles, "I thought you and your girl devoured it?"

"Now you know I wouldn't do that to you. How'd your meeting with JT go?" Ania walks over to the counter in the kitchen and Larenz has his eyes on her behind and the thong that is slightly covered by her silk gown hugging her just the right way. She picks up her camera that she keeps at the ready and she starts to take pictures of Larenz getting situated and comfortable in the house.

Larenz says, "C'mon now, will you ever have enough pictures of me?"

She says, "No, plus you said that last time. You better act like you know what this is. This is my life and I'm behind on my pics of you for the month."

Ania has the camera on continuous mode and Larenz is not feeling the nonstop flash in his eyes. He says, "So, you're telling me, these pictures are going to be stock photos or something like that? You can't have me up in no stock joints?"

She laughs at his comment. "No."

"Well, you have to have enough pictures of me by now, after all these years."

"I don't know why you're playing Larenz because the pictures I have of you are going to be left for our grandchildren."

"If my grandkids take the time to look at all the pics you've taken of me, after all these years, they damn sure ain't going to have a life of their own and I can just wonder what it will do to their mental."

"Be quiet and smile." He does and his smiles are fake and silly and Ania doesn't mind one bit. "If my grandkids are like me they'll love all of the pics." She puts the camera down. "So, tell me about the meeting?"

"Oh, the meeting was straight, just have to keep on top of this commercial building. Have to keep things in order if we want to stay on schedule with the rehab."

"So, everything's good?"

"Yeah, good. But after my meeting Calvin came in and he was distraught about some things he's dealing with."

"Really, is Kris okay?"

"Yeah, she's good."

"Good."

"It's Cam though."

"What is it?"

"He borrowed some money from Calvin months ago promised he would pay it back but hasn't and the money Calvin gave him was for their anniversary trip to the Bahamas."

"Now Cam knows better than that. How old is he now, twenty-three, twenty-four? That is not a good look."

"Yeah, it's a whack situation, so I'm going to give him a little bonus check you know. Show him we appreciate him so he can take Kris as planned no worries."

Ania walks over to him. "Really? Now that's nice of you. I mean what other boss you know of would do something like that? You're a real boss. I am here for it, long as you don't forget about our trip."

"Never that."

"I can't lie I'm getting anxious to leave. So, make it happen boss man."

"I don't know when, but you just be ready."

"Well, just know that since we are talking about vacations, and families and sons. I spoke with our one and only child earlier today and just so you know, he wants to have his party down at some new club all his friends have been going to."

"What do you mean? Doesn't he want to have the party at our place like we always do?"

"No, Larenz that's the problem, he always has it there. I can't blame him, it's time for him to change it up a bit."

"So, how much is this change going to cost? That's what I want to know."

Ania says, "I don't know, let's just let our only born be happy." And just like it was meant to be Sade's *Nothing Can Come Between Us* comes on over her playlist and Ania puts her arms up in the air and her hips are moving back and forth in perfect unison. "Oh, my goodness that's my song. See they don't make music like this anymore." All the wine and drinks of the night have caught up with Ania and she has her sexy, freak nasty rolled into one real nice in front of Larenz then she remembers as she continues her dance. "Oh, yeah I invited Jill and Kerry to perform at the club whenever they decide. They're going through some record company drama and I told them they are welcome."

"That's cool. They doin' alright? When did you talk to her about performing?"

"Tonight, at the club. We came over had a few drinks and something to munch on. Calvin picked us up. I guess you were in your meeting with JT. I would have told you but didn't want to disturb you since it seemed so urgent."

Larenz picks up the camera and takes a couple of shots of Ania and she is feeling every beat of the music and turns around closes her eyes, giving him free access to her backside and continues to dance. Larenz is blunt. "Hey, did you happen to run into anybody at the club tonight you haven't seen in a while?"

Ania's eyes open and she stops cold. "No, sure didn't."

"Oh really," Larenz says and places the camera back down.

Ania turns around to face Larenz. "Nope, just me and Jill. Chatting about old times and Nicole getting better." She walks over to Larenz nice and slow. "So, are you ready to finish what we started earlier?"

The music stops and Larenz looks at his wife up and down with his drink still in his hand. "You know what baby, I'm good. Need to get some sleep, I have a big day tomorrow."

She places her hand on her hip. "Are you serious?"

"Yeah, I think I'll sleep in the guest room. I need some really good rest I have a big day tomorrow."

"But it's Saturday?"

"I know, we're grinding anyway. Nite."

–

The very same night Jill is standing behind Kerry undetected while he is deep into working his magic playing his bass guitar. It's like he's making love to it as she has never witnessed anyone in all of her years in music make the instrument sound so sweet. He doesn't even recognize her behind him, he is so much into his musical assault. When he finishes, the room is as quiet as an opera singer hitting her last note in the largest of halls. Jill walks up to Kerry from behind and runs her hand over his shoulder.

"Sounding good baby," she says, "Is that something new?"

"Yeah, new to someone my love, but not to me, I've had that inside of me for some time now, it's just now coming out."

She smiles. "I heard that black man. Need to record that, that's for sure."

"Well, you know what they say, twelve notes is twelve notes."

"Say it louder, for the children in the back because you, my brother, were playing all those notes, you understand me?"

He smiles. "Right, right thank you baby." Then he starts to fidget on the bass just running up and down the frets. "So, what's good?"

"Not much, just got back from the club, chit chatting with Ania."

"Everybody good?" He is still strumming the frets of his bass.

"Yes, they're fine."

"Cool." All of a sudden Kerry, hears something he likes on his bass and points to Jill to listen. He finds a groove and points to her to join him with her undeniable voice.

She smiles. "Oh, okay, I like that. Is that how we're doing it tonight Mr. Kerry?" She continues to listen to him tear the bass up and then she joins and it's jazzy, funky, her voice golden and melting. "*It seemed like you…you knew you were going to see me...today. It seemed like you…knew that I would be right in place. If I would guess the thing you'd say…oh Baby…if I would of knew you'd be so cool when I seen ya baby….then I woulda got prepared for our interaction baby…how'd you know I'd be there baby….sha…bee…bid it bee, oh bee, baby, how did you know…oh, how did you know…*" Then Kerry shuts it down with a nasty riff at the end.

Kerry says, "Oh my goodness, where'd all that come from?"

Jill says, "Just life, some funny but odd life happenings today." Then she looks around at all his music equipment. "Tell me you recorded that?"

He turns the recording off. "Gotdamn right."

She smiles, "Twelve notes, baby."

He sets down his bass. "Tell me what's going on?"

Jill says, "It was the craziest thing. We were walking in the club and some guy that Ania used to be involved with just came out of nowhere and took her by surprise."

Kerry says, "He came 'outta nowhere? That's a bad nigga."

"Don't start. But the way her eyes popped out her head. At one point in her life, she cared something about this guy. Even if it was an itty, bitty bit, she cared."

"Some love from the past nonsense, huh?"

"Yeah, it was Bill Cash."

"Hold up, the record label guy who pimps his performers and makes millions?"

"The one and only, all Gee'd up and pimped out for all to see."

"Now, that's interesting."

"She told me; it was before they even moved here. Some deep dark past flow, that she always said she buried but I don't know. You know how looks and eyes are."

Kerry thinks about it. "Nah, baby you're reaching."

"You think?"

He nods his head yes.

She says, "Any…who, what're we going to do about this recording contract?"

"What do you mean? We're not going to do anything. Now, if you want to sell yourself short, go'head but ain't nobody getting me shackled up in a 360 deal."

"Baby look, it's only for one album."

"Look, the record companies think because the structure of actual sales have gone down, they have to put their hand in the artist pocket. Nobody pimping me, and everybody already knows that, so why are they even asking?"

"Cause, they want you involved, beloved."

"Well, they want me involved they better miss me with that 360 trash." Kerry moves over to the drums then starts to tap on the hardhat. Jill sits and listens for a few seconds but she is really thinking about how his decision is keeping them from getting some quick fast money then after a few minutes she gets up and walks out.

Ride 2 Work

Even though it's the weekend it doesn't stop Larenz from grinding. It has always been one of his busiest days at the club, and he and JT decide to squeeze an additional real estate meeting at the commercial site. He wakes up on the move, ready for business. When he walks into the kitchen, Ania and their son, Jacob, are enjoying one another's company.

"Morning family," Larenz says.

Ania smiles and looks him over.

"What's up pop?" Jacob says. "Look at you bruh, not even eight yet and you're already making moves. Okay, I see you."

"What's good son? Busy day today, I have to go over to see the commercial building with JT."

Ania says, "Want some coffee?"

"No thanks." Larenz says back. Ania gives him another wondering look as Larenz turns to his son. "So, I hear you're trying to branch out a bit, by having your party across town somewhere, J?"

Jacob looks at Ania and she says, "What, I didn't know it was a secret?"

"Yeah, no hard feelings pop, I just wanted to do something different this year, you know, switch up a little, with the big two-five coming up-it's time for change, brand identity, and thangs. Plus, the ladies like to see you switch it up sometimes–you'd be surprised; it keeps you relevant. The club is called Marbles." Ania gives Jacob his plate and tells Larenz she's getting him some coffee and toast, and he agrees.

"Marbles? The ladies, huh?"

Jacob smiles. "That's right."

"What you know about that?"

"Bruh, I'm rolling up to two-five, I know more than you can remember."

Ania laughs.

Larenz gives her a look. "Don't forget son, I am half the reason you're here and look at you–so you know my work. And since you're talking about the ladies, I was just thinking the other day, you have never in your life brought a lady friend over for us to meet, but you're always talking about them. Sup with that?"

"I already told you pop. Rule number one in the handbook, never bring them home."

Larenz and Ania ask, "never?" at the same time.

"You heard me, never ever, ever. Look, nowadays is nothing like when y'all were coming up. It's levels to this thing now. See, if I were coming up when you were and bringing them over to meet you, you'd be like, damn son, you need to pick one because they're all so fine, but those days are over."

Larenz says, "Oh, they're over? You can't let your own father meet your girl?"

"That's the point, she needs to be *my* girl. If not, you might end up getting robbed or something like that."

Larenz and Ania ask, "robbed?" Again, at the same time.

Ania says, "What are you talking about?"

"I'm telling you. This is how it goes nowadays. These females will come over your house, check it out and if they see things that are worth money they'll tell their people and the next thing you know you don't have it anymore."

Ania says, "No…."

Jacob says, "Yes, ma it's exactly how the game is run these days. So, I'm basically protecting you."

Larenz taps his son on the shoulder and smiles. "That's crazy, I thought you didn't bring them around because you like them big, you know thick as they call it. Not that I have anything against that, I just figured you didn't want me to know what you're into yet."

"Stop tryin' me pops."

Larenz smiles. "Just saying, baby boy, just saying. I mean, like I said, I've never seen what you're into, my brother. What's the secret-ya heard—as you youngsters say."

"Well, I might be introducing you soon."

Larenz says, "Oh really, that means you like her then right?"

"Yes, that's what it means."

Ania says, "Who is she?"

Jacob's grin is wide. "Later for all that. You'll like her though, I'm sure of that."

Ania says, "Dang, can't even get to hear a little about her?"

"Patience, mama, patience."

"I'll give you some patience alright," she lets him know then gives Larenz his coffee and a slice of toast with grape jelly, just before they all hear JT blow on the horn outside.

"Well, that's JT, gotta' go."

"Have a good day," Ania says.

"Thanks, you too," Larenz says right before he grabs his things and is out the door.

Jacob picks up on something. "Hey, you two cool?"

Ania says, "Umm, hmm cool as a fan, cool as a fan."

–

JT has his eyes on Larenz as he walks out the door, holding his coffee cup and strolling down the driveway to the car. Then JT starts to adjust the settings on the radio so that he can hear it better. Larenz gets in the car greets JT with good morning and JT mumbles back, and Larenz is pretty sure he said good morning back to him. JT puts the car in gear without another word and takes off as Larenz zooms in on what's so damn important on the radio. Some guy is doing an interview with the host of a morning show talking about high-earning men and the women that can have a high earner and those who can't, and then it goes to commercial. Larenz says, "Bruh, I know you're not listening to that garbage, you don't even have a woman."

"I know, I have women. Make it plural, my brother then keep it plural."

"Oh, okay Don Juan."

"No, I'm serious about this. This brother sounds on point to me because we're high earners. We are doing damn well and you know how it is out here. It makes a brother really look at motives and all when they meet someone new."

Larenz says, "I don't know but you're right about one thing– I am a high earner, but I'm not out here for the streets like that."

"I understand but just think about it. What man with money that "you" know is going to go out his mind and lug around someone else's kids instead of having a comfortable single situation? And please don't say, the quarterback everyone knows and loves because that is the only situation like that any of us know about on the big stage, plus that queen is fine as a muthafuka'. Matter of fact, I would seriously think about taking care of her best friend's kids too, to get with her."

Larenz laughs a bit. "Not her best friend's kids? She's that fine too you, huh?"

"Absolutely."

Larenz takes his eyes off the road and looks at JT and points to the radio. "Look here man, I think this guy is talking from a player's perspective. Someone out there in the game." Larenz keeps his eyes on JT as he's driving and JT notices.

JT says, "Oh, you're talking about me?"

"Yes sir, you're in the game aren't you?"

"Yeah, I'm out here and forty pounds lighter in ten months only done with hard work."

"I see you. I see the workouts getting you right."

"But it's touch and go, right now with the ladies man."

"Touch and go?"

"Yeah, I touch, then go. I'm not trying to decipher whose playing games because I gotta' bag. I mean we're doing well; thank GOD and we keep paper. But just think about the brothers who have the deepest pockets. They are getting it at all angles, married or not bruh, and I think it is damn near impossible in this day and age to just be with one woman. You have to have some strong love or blinders on looking straight ahead every day."

"Oh, so now you're talking about– me?" Larenz says.

JT looks over at him. "Yes, yes, exactly I'm talking about you–my brother. You fit the description."

"It's a matter of perspective. I mean you have to find a woman from jump and go through somethings with her to realize she's the one. I mean she does too."

JT says, "Oh, you're talking about putting in that time. Lots of women say they don't want to waste their time."

"See, those are the ones to stay away from."

"Why?"

"I mean, what's the rush? Finding someone is way more than finding someone, ya dig?"

"Oh, so you're about to get all poetic up in here. I mean it has been a while since you have. You want me to swing by the club so you can drop a poem?"

"You're funny. They should have you on this sham of a show telling jokes right after the commercial or something. But think about it, is it really wasted time though?"

"Lots of women out here, certainly think so."

"Listen man, you need time. And that's why I say, if she doesn't have time then you should stay clear from her. In my book being together with someone ain't about no time; at least until you're years in. But it's about a connection. For me a connection does not equate to time."

JT says, "Negro, what?"

Larenz shakes his head and laughs JT off, and then he turns the radio down when the relationship guru JT is listening to comes back on. "Look man, that time excuse gets no points with me. I mean you can have the best time with someone that you ever have had in your life. You know like moments and the like. But if you don't have a connection, I'm talking about when they know when you're going through something. When they really know you and you know them, how they love, how you feel about things, how you react when they are feeling a certain kind of way and if they like you for any of it." Larenz pauses. "Time? When you are with someone you're feeling, you lose track of time– if you don't, you ain't got nothing bruh."

JT looks over at Larenz. "Damn, can I use that B? I'm for real? The next occasion one of these honey-dips tell me they don't want to waste their time, that's exactly what I'm going to say."

Larenz shakes his head and starts to laugh. "Man get yourself a life."

JT presses him. "I'm serious, write that down for me."

"Yeah, right. How about I just put it in an email?"

"No, serious– I need that."

"Just giving my perspective, bruh, that's all I'm doing." Larenz gets a text right after. It's Ania and she wants to know if he is okay and why he's being so short with her. He stares at the text for a beat or two then texts back that everything is fine.

JT looks over at him. "You good?"

"Yeah man, I'm good."

"Don't give me that. Who was that?"

"Ania."

"She good?"

"Yeah, just wants to know if I am."

"Ohh, that connection vibe, huh?"

"Yeah, man."

"What y'all connecting about?"

"Bruh, you're all in my business?"

"We ain't been all business in damn near twenty-years, what's good?"

Larenz doesn't answer right away. "Okay look, you know that pinhead nigga that came into my office last night offering to put his act on our stage and we keep all the money on the receipts?"

"Cash, right?"

"Yeah."

JT says, "You know I never discuss business in front of ops, but quiet as it's kept, I would have put a hold on that offer and told him I would think on it. It's money B."

"And ordinarily I would have, you know that. But I know him from Chicago. Not just on some cordial whoot-de-whoot. He was part of my click in the Chi– I hung out with his ass."

JT looks over at Larenz. "Oh…really?"

"And so did, Ania."

JT says with way more passion this time, "Ohh…really?"

"Yeah man, can you freeze that "oh really?" Check this out, since you are my chief finance officer, slash, security and graduate of The Central State University."

"That's me, go Marauders." JT blurts out whenever his alma mater is mentioned.

"I've had something on my mind behind all that too."

"What's up?"

"Remember he told us he had spoken to Ania last night?"

"Yeah, yeah he said he ran into her, but I didn't see her that night until you rolled back the shades and she was sitting with Jill's fine ass."

"Stay focused on my situation bruh. So, I asked her about it when I got home."

"What you mean asked her?"

"When I got home last night, we were vibing a lil' bit."

"Oh, I see, getting back to the earlier days happenings, I interrupted?"

"Whatever, so I asked her plain as day if there was anyone at the club she saw that she hadn't in a while, and she straight up told me no, when I know good damn well that she saw this sucker that she used to kick it with."

"So, what'd you say?"

"Nothin' not a damn word."

"What?"

"I just went to bed and thought about how I should approach it because I'm not down with the drama in my life right now, ya dig. I have way too much going on, to be wondering why my girl, felt the need to straight-up lie to me."

"That is a question that needs to be answered, unless she…"

"Unless she what?"

JT doesn't answer, he just keeps his eyes on the road and reaches for the radio. "Let's see what this guy is talking now?"

Larenz turns it back down. "Unless what, JT?"

JT looks at him. "Unless she likes what she saw or has other plans with his ass."

"What?"

"Look, I'm just being real. If she saw him and didn't tell you, why the hell you think she didn't say anything? Especially if she use to see him?"

Larenz thinks on it. “Exactly. It’s a good question and I just want to know why she couldn’t tell me she saw him?”

“Only she knows bro, only she knows.”

Larenz is really searching and his voice drops a bit and JT barely hears him. “I mean someone in your past pop up and you act like they didn’t and lie about it when asked about it?” Larenz truly doesn’t understand and nods his head back and forth.

JT tries to shake him out of it. “Look, we’re here now. Can’t worry about it. Get your game hat on and let’s handle this business.”

Hey There

Ania sends Larenz another text, but this time he doesn't answer her back directly. She briefly imagines her man is with JT already handling their business properly at the commercial property and wishes him well. Right after, she puts on her Chanel rectangle shades and smiles at what looks to be a mother and daughter walking the grounds of the mental facility her best friend, Nicole, has been holed up in for much too long. She gets out the car to go inside to see Nicole for their weekly visit. She's better now about going inside but she always has to prepare herself with a few deep breaths to help with her anxiety of the visit. As Ania walks down the sidewalk leading up to the entrance she is bewildered to see Bill Cash coming out the building, donning his sunglasses and strutting like he is truly running it out on the streets. He notices her so suddenly that Ania doesn't even have the chance to turn around and walk in the opposite direction if she wants to.

He says, "Oh my goodness, oh my goodness, the sun is really shining bright today. Hey, Ms. Ania gurrl…."

Ania is confused as hell. "Hey, uh Bill, what're you doing here?"

He smiles. "Well, good day to you too sunshine."

Ania still is baffled, the look on her face is like she just heard a verdict of another black man being shot by the police and watching the asshole who shot him walk free or something. "Okay, good morning. Like, what're you doing here, Bill?"

"I just come from seeing our girl. Just to say hello, you know."

"Our girl? You mean Nicole?"

"Yeah, don't be confused, because I see you're blurred right now. See, me and Nicole we have managed to keep in touch all these years through her family and everything back home you know. I mean sometimes I help her out when need be."

Ania tries to look through Bill's darkened shades to look at his eyes to see what the hell kind of deception he is on. "Oh, that's interesting. Funny, she never mentioned it to me, and I talk to her almost every day and see her at least once a week."

He pauses then says, "Hmm, I don't know why either? Might be one of the reasons she's up in here, you know? But she's good, really sharp, told me, she was moving in with you and the fam' as soon as they say it's a go."

Ania slowly says, "Yes… yes, she is."

There is a quick awkward moment and silence takes over the conversation and they both can feel it and then Bill points over to a nearby bench a few steps away.

He says, "Hey, you gotta' minute?"

Ania looks over at the bench then at him and takes a deep breath and decides, "Yeah, sure."

They walk over to the bench and sit down. Bill waits for her to sit first and afterwards Ania checks her phone to see if Larenz just so happened to text her back and waits for what Bill has to say.

Bill doesn't hesitate. "Listen, you know it was really good running into you the other night." Ania acknowledges she hears him with a nod of her head. "You know, I just want to say that it's been some years since we have sat down and had a conversation but I told myself, if I ever get a chance I want to say, I apologize for any harm I imposed in your life back in the day."

Ania really doesn't even want to respond but says, "Okay, thanks, appreciate it."

He smiles and his voice raises a bit. "Now, your husband, on the other hand." Then he starts to laugh.

"What do you mean?"

"I'm just saying, when I went back to his office and he was sitting in the back room, with his security guy."

"Security?"

"Yeah, the big black dude, he didn't say anything, but when he got the vibe L wasn't feeling me, he unrelaxed himself, if that's even a word."

Ania rolls her eyes not believing she is entertaining this conversation. "Yeah, it's a word."

"Good, well I went in to say hello, and L– he like showed me no hometown love. After all these years. I mean do you know, if he still has beef with me?"

"Look, I don't know."

"Well, I offered an olive branch. You know, I've done pretty good in the music business, right?"

"Yes, I know, I see you."

"Well, I offered to let my new group pack the house down at Nickels so they can get some of the ATL love and he flat out denied me. I mean, I offered one-hundred percent take of the door and everything because truth of the matter, I don't need that. My new group needs the exposure that word of mouth only The A can provide."

"Well, he didn't mention it to me, so I can't really speak on it. Besides Larenz is running things, has been, and always will be. But hey, I'm sure Nicole enjoyed your visit." Ania stands up.

Bill says, "Well, yeah okay. Look, I'm gonna' be here for a minute to try to get my act some of this Atlanta love before I fly out to Monaco for a little vacation."

The destination catches her off guard since it is where Larenz has promised to take her. "Monaco? How nice."

"Yeah, just a little something I do just to get away, you know how it is."

"Yeah, I know. Nice seeing you." Ania turns and starts to walk away. She can see that Bill has knocked his glasses down to his nose and is standing with his eyes on her through the reflection of the glass door she is walking toward; then, he turns and walks away.

Ania signs into the facility, and just by walking inside, it pushes her anxiety to another level. It has been the worst part for Ania because it scares her so much. One time during a visit, a patient, who should have been on lockdown, found a way out of his room and made a disturbance she will never forget, before security ran him down, tackled the distraught man then restrained him before he could hurt anyone. So, she is always on alert, as she is this time, walking towards Nicole's room. As she walks past the rooms in the hallway that have cream-colored cinderblock walls, a patient standing in his doorway staring into the hallway startles her, forcing her to pick up her pace; when she turns the corner to continue to Nicole's room, she almost collides with another man walking on the wrong side of the hallway. She lets out a slight scream and puts her hands out so they don't collide. They both stop, take a quick glance at one another and he steps to his right and keeps it moving. She only has a few more steps until she gets to Nicole's room, and when she does Nicole is standing, wearing a floral sundress looking out the window. Nicole turns around waves Ania in, and they hug and are truly happy to see one another.

"Girl, I heard you scream in the hallway," she giggles a bit. "G-man must be out there walking on the wrong side again."

"G-man? Why do you call him that?"

"Everybody does, he's always going room to room asking everyone if they have any gin for him. So, they call him G-man."

"Okay then…. and yes, G-man scared me half to death." They laugh.

"Trust me when I tell you, that negro should be in here for real." They laugh a bit more and Nicole has turned to look out the window again. "Hey, you see that bench? The one you were sitting on, while you were talking to Bill?"

Ania is kind of surprised. "Oh, you saw that, huh?"

"Sure did."

"What about it?"

"Well, I've sat there plenty of times with my thoughts. Thoughts of when I was going to get out of here or even, if I could get out." Ania rubs her back understanding her struggle full strength because she has been through it since day one with her. "But it's something about that bench."

"Oh, is it, now?"

"Umm…hmm it's a revealer of truth. I know you didn't know that when you sat down talking with Bill. But sis, that bench there will release and reveal things that you never wanted to let go of in your mind just by sitting on it and talking. It brings things to the table that you have suppressed so long in your life that you almost forget all about them. I think it's because it's really the only place to sit out there. I mean, I've sat there time and time again and I've watched people sit out there and talk and just think they are generally shooting the breeze. But, BaeBae, that bench right there? Too many souls have sat there, releasing their inner thoughts and they have soaked deep down inside that wood and have a life of their own all together and guess what?"

"What's that?"

"Two things are for sure and one is as true as it leaves my mouth. Once you sit there and talk and have thoughts, whether suppressed or expressed, you either get weaker or you get stronger. But best believe it will be one or the other and just pray that you can handle whatever it is." She turns and looks at Ania, then they both turn and look at the bench again.

Business Run

Larenz and JT are walking away from their commercial property. All you can hear are their shoes striking the concrete pavement. The car doors open and shut as JT starts up his ride.

Larenz says, "Can you believe that man?"

JT says, "Oh yeah, I believe it. And the thing about it, I don't think it's about the building at all. It's about us."

"Exactly, always is."

"You know the story. Two brothers walking in, and they already know we're making a profit off this commercial joint. So, you know they're going to try and stop it or delay it as much as possible so we can't get to the bag."

"Or until we decide to grease them hands a bit. You think I wasn't picking up on their hints?"

"Exactly."

"But this ain't the old days bruh. We here, and we're not giving away money after we have busted our asses this far. Forget that and forget them," Larenz decides. JT agrees. "So, how much will it cost to make these so-called codes disappear? We can still make this happen right? We can get things up to code?"

"Yeah man, they're messing with us. They're not even the actual inspectors. Those guys are a private company just giving us a look see, to tell us what the real inspectors might find and they're also locked in with the city inspectors. So, they're making deals all day. I mean, if we give them some cash to try to fix these items, they'll turn around and let the city inspectors know we are handing out cash like skittles, then the city guys are going to want a kick. Hell yeah, we have the money to get this done, but like I said, more money coming in would be good for any incidentals so that we don't have to cut into our profit."

"Yeah, sounds good," Larenz decides.

JT looks over at Larenz. "Maybe you should take that pin-headed muthafucka, as you called him, up on his deal. That could give us some buffer money. And you know me, I hate to walk away from money anyway. I mean, he has already offered so let's just find out how much he's willing to come off of and let's triple it. Yeah, that's paper right there."

"I feel you, tax him to use the space."

"Yeah man, I Googled him, he has it."

"So, you looked the man up?"

"Yeah, it's my job ain't it? A man walks into the establishment talking about he is ready to drop some bread and offers you an opportunity with monetary gain for himself on the backend? That is a man you vet properly– don't you think?"

"You're right. You're right." Larenz thinks on it. "But hell nah, you don't know this guy like I do."

JT gives Larenz a look. Trying to understand but not getting it. "So, you're holding back on some crisis that happened– how long ago?"

"Years, I'm talking before I moved here, way over twenty. But the fact of the matter is, his kind don't change. I know where he's from and what he's on, and it doesn't change."

"Well, since you know how he vibes, and I'm just throwing this out there 'cause I was a badass too, over twenty-years ago, I mean people change–that my brother you have to know."

"I know it."

"And since you took home the prize, you got the girl that means you should have nothing to worry about. Don't you got Ania?"

"Hell yeah, I got her."

"Well, there's no problem then. Call his ass up and make

the deal."

Larenz doesn't answer right back because he notices the sign Marbles as they are riding. "Yo, yo pull over right here."

JT wants to be sure. "In here, on the right?"

"Yeah, right here."

"For what?"

"This is where Jacob wants to have his party. I gotta go rent this joint out." Larenz looks around and checks the place out as JT pulls into the lot. After a brief discussion on whether or not JT should bring his pistol with him, Larenz decides against it. Still, JT stuffs it in his jacket, and they go inside. When they walk in, just like any club worth attending, a cleaning crew is getting things ready for their nighttime traffic. As they stand looking around, they are approached by a young female.

She says, "Yes, can I help you?"

JT defers to Larenz. "Wondering if the manager is available so I can set up a party?"

"Okay sure, if you would just wait here for a second, I'll go get exactly who you need to talk to."

Larenz and JT are waiting giving the club a glance over and they both peer at the DJ booth and can tell right away that the club sets a high priority on DJ's in opposition to Nickels because Nickels is all about the stage and ambiance. They notice the young lady speak to a woman who has her back towards them, then she turns around and starts to approach them. As she gets closer Larenz squints his eyes and is flabbergasted.

"Lisa?"

She smiles, “Hello, Larenz, it’s been a long time. Welcome to Club Marbles.”

Larenz is confused and wondering but still smiling. “Wow, Lisa, yeah, yes, you’re right-it’s been a long time. I didn’t..”

“Surprising huh, seeing me here?”

JT is following their awkward conversation with a smile on his face.

“Yeah, of course. I had no idea. Do you live here?”

“Yes.”

“That’s crazy, for how long?” JT clears his throat and Larenz catches on. “Oh, my bad. Lisa, this is my business partner, JT. JT, this is Lisa, an old friend from back in the day.”

JT says, “My pleasure.”

She says, “Nice to meet you, as well.”

JT tells them, “Look, I’ll just have a look around while you two catch up, if that’s okay?”

“Sure, would you like something to drink?”

“That would be nice,” he says.

Lisa raises her hand over to the young lady that greeted them into the club and she walks over and waits for instructions. “Would you take Mr. JT over to the bar and get him his drink of choice?”

JT walks over to the bar with the young lady and Lisa and Larenz go through the maze of an awkward moment. Lisa says, “So, Larenz you’re planning a party? And to answer your question, I’ve been here quite some time, twenty-three, twenty-four years, but who’s counting anymore.”

"Wow, that long?" Larenz shakes his head struggling somehow to trace the years.

She interrupts his thoughts. "And about that party?"

He says, "Oh, yeah, it's for my son. He's turning twenty-five and this is the spot that he swears it needs to be so, here I am to make it happen. It's my present to him."

"Doesn't want to have it at your spot, huh?"

"My– spot?"

"Yes, your spot."

"You know about my spot?"

"Yes, I know about your spot."

Larenz is not sure if she is being coy or not and says, "Ahh, yeah, right."

"So, when is his birthday?"

"His birthday, uh, it's in a few days. It's on the ninth, yeah September ninth."

Lisa smiles. "Same day as mine, imagine that."

Larenz goes back into his memory bank again and tries like hell to remember, but he can't, and it shows all over his face; then he tries to lie about it, "Wow, it sure is."

"Don't worry, you always forgot my birthday Larenz no biggie."

There is another pause. "So, can you handle it? He'll probably pack your club out, he's somewhat that guy around here," Larenz says.

"Is that right? Just like his dad."

"Nah, he's on a whole different level."

"Well, I will be happy to host him and his party. Can set him up, give him a nice VIP section, matter of fact because he's your son. I'll give him two VIP sections, because I know all about those different levels."

"That would be great."

"Done."

"Good."

Lisa says, "Have him call me, so that I can get his bottle preference, he has my number."

Larenz is perplexed. "Wait, he has your number?"

"Yes, Jacob's dating my daughter. Nice seeing you again, Larenz." Then she turns around and walks away.

JT walks over to him afterwards. "Do I need to pick you up and carry your ass to the car, or what? Because you my brother look shook."

–

When they finally make it back to the car, Larenz checks his phone and is reading a text. "Well, looks like today is the day."

JT says, "For what?"

"Ania got the clearance to bring Nicole home to live with us."

"That's huge man, I can't wait to see her."

"Yeah, me too, She's good people for sure."

JT pulls onto the main street from the parking lot and when they were settled in traffic he looks over at Larenz. "What was that inside?"

"What do you mean?"

"The club owner, no doubt in my mind you knew her in a different life?"

Larenz takes a deep breath then explains. "We kicked it back in the day."

JT smiles. "I bet you did, because she had you dazed and wobbling from side to side−my boy."

"Bruh we use to kick it. Kind of serious for a quick minute, but I held it at bay. We dated though and I was definitely surprised to see her, I cannot lie."

"Oh, okay, now I see."

"Crazy," Larenz explains.

"So, are you going to tell Ania about this unplanned sighting?"

Larenz turns to JT. "No, hell no, why would I do that?"

"I'm just asking because you're mad at her for seeing someone and not letting you know about it. Ain't that the story you told me?"

"Don't start with me JT. I'm not talking about that right now, ya dig?"

JT laughs a bit. "My brother, you gotta' attack it now 'cause she's going to find out. And if you don't tell her about it, she's going to think you're hiding it for a reason, plus some other mess along with it, and she'll just get unbearable to be around. If you want her to do some shit, you better be ready to do it too."

"Well, it's already too late for her. She had her chance to tell me."

"Oh, yeah?"

"That's right because I asked her and she lied about it. Put it like this if she asks about it, I'll tell her. If she doesn't, I won't." JT looks at him a few times while driving. "Eyes on the road, eyes on the road." Then he pushes down on his phone and waits.

"I got this. I been driving before you even thought about getting behind the wheel." JT lets him know.

Now Larenz is on the phone. "Hey, Jacob it's me. Can you give me a call asap? I need to talk to you about something." Then he clicks his phone off. JT looks at him again then back on the road as it has started to rain and he turns on the windshield wipers. Larenz says, "Do you know, back at the club o'girl told me, my son was dating her daughter?"

"My nephew?"

"Yeah man, do you think she is just messing with me?" Larenz thinks for a few seconds, "Nah, she couldn't be, she mentioned my son by his name bruh."

JT says, "Have you ever met her? Have you seen her or what?"

"My son doesn't bring females to see me man. He's always talking this; they'll help steal all of your belongings shit."

"Crazy man, your old girl comes and sets up shop in The A you know nothing about it and now she tells you her daughter is dating your son? Crazy."

"I know right?" Larenz looks over at JT then outside as the rain starts to come down harder.

Raindrops

The entire city of Atlanta is getting rain and it hasn't let up one bit since Ania and Nicole put her things in the car and left the facility once and for all. Nicole has her eyes pierced on the downpour and then turns to Ania while she drives.

Ania notices her gaze. "You good?"

"Yes, I'm fine, just a little surprised that the doctor said I could leave. I am so grateful…."

"So, how does it feel, you must have so many emotions right now?"

"I do, everything just looks so different." Nicole continues to look around. "Tell me, exactly how long was I in that place?"

Ania keeps her eyes on the road and doesn't answer right back. She doesn't know if she should speak on the past, just gloss over things or tell her the truth and move on. She says, "You were there a little over two years, twenty-six months—that's it."

"I see you're trying to lessen the blow," Nicole chuckles. "Still a long time. You know, I never really even counted the days and time I was inside that place. That definitely would have messed with my head. Now, I get a chance to be done finally and do the work to get better, but things have changed; none of this is looking familiar to me-I just need to get my bearings back."

"Baby don't worry about it, there is no rush; everything will come back to you soon enough."

Ania runs over one of the many damn Atlanta potholes. She has to hit the brakes a bit before she goes through what looks like a river in the road because the drains are stopped up. Ania keeps moving without a word about the street conditions because she is very familiar. Nicole says, "Yeah, but what if I don't want it to come back?"

Ania looks over to her real quick so she can keep her eyes on the road. "What do you mean?"

"I'm just saying, those memories, those times, whatever I was going through, I don't want to remember what took me away from my daily life and the things I love. I would just rather not and start with this clean slate and learn everything again, like it's my first time seeing it."

"Well, that's exactly what you can do then. It's a wonderful idea. Do what's comfortable for you. Start anew, do something fresh, live your life girl."

Nicole turns to Ania. "Wow, you sound just like Bill."

"I do?"

"Yeah, he is so full of energy like that. He's one person for sure that still has some fire under him and likes to make things happen. I really respect him for that."

"Yes, he seems to be certainly busy. When we were talking he told me, he was going on a vacation soon."

"Yeah, to Monaco, that's what he told me."

"He surprised me when he let me know you two have been in touch."

"He's always been in touch. Always making sure I am okay."

"Why didn't you tell me?"

"Because, I didn't want to bring him up to you. I always like to see how you and Larenz move and there was no reason to bring his ass up to you, that's the only reason."

Ania smiles. "Girl, you did right, believe me. But I have to say a vacation does sound nice."

–

Larenz and JT return to the club and are in the office after rushing inside to get out the rain. Calvin knocks on the door, enters, sits down a couple of coffees on the desk, and then wants to know if Larenz needs him to pick anything else up.

"Nah, bruh you need to get ready to be going, right? What time are you leaving for all that beautiful sunshine and relaxation?"

Calvin says, "In the morning, can't wait."

JT chimes in, "Awwww… yeah, that's what I'm talkin' about, enjoy yourself my brother, enjoy yourself with your lady and I really do mean that."

"Look, I appreciate y'all man, Larenz for the bonus and JT for picking up the hotel expense."

Larenz looks at JT. "You did that? See, that's love man."

JT says, "Gotta' have him right, commitment is special man when you can find it, especially these days and we've watched this brother be a man all these years. He has handled his life as a man should– taking care of his family, treating his lady right, never any problems at the workplace, so yeah, enjoy it. Enjoy yourself to the fullest you've earned it, my brother."

Larenz takes a sip of his coffee then says, "Hell yeah, relish the moment with your wife and make special memories. So, you'll be in the air in the morning, huh?"

Calvin smiles. "Yes sir, eight in the morning."

Larenz says, "I bet your ass ain't even all the way packed yet, are you?"

"Ain't taking much, I'm going to be laying out."

JT says, "I heard that."

"Well, we're good here, so go home." Larenz pushes him away with both hands in the air. "Go get ready to go, go man, take the day."

Calvin isn't so sure. "But we're about to get busy up in here in a few hours?"

"Trust me, we're good," Larenz says.

Calvin doesn't hesitate, "Okay, cool. I will see y'all good brothers when I get back."

Larenz and JT dap Calvin up and he moves towards the door. When he shuts the door completely, they sit down and start to enjoy their coffee, and then there is a knock.

Calvin sticks his head inside. "Yo, you have a visitor." Then he opens the door wider where they can see Bill standing dripping wet from the rain.

Off the rip, Bill says, "Damn, gotdamn security in this joint tight- ain't it?" Bill is looking Calvin up and down like they might have had words on the other side of the door or something.

Calvin looks at Larenz. "He good?"

Larenz tells him, yes, and Calvin steps away from the door, gives Bill a look then walks away. Bill looks around at the surroundings in the office and he swipes off the rain drops on his clothes. "This here takes some time to get use to; got me drenched like I been hit with a gotdamn super soaker or something." He looks around, "Help me out, can I get a paper towel or something to wipe it down or what?" JT grabs a small napkin sitting next to his coffee, stands up, and gives it to Bill; he looks at it, then back at JT at his nerve. "I would say thanks, but I'm not." Then he mumbles, "Giving me this little ass piece of nothing." Larenz and JT have yet to say a word because they are evaluating him.

"So, you called a brother? I understand you want to talk and I hope it's about the deal I presented to you. Just to let you know, 'cause we go way back, I've presented the same deal, but just not so sweet, to a few other clubs and they all were a little more accepting than you, Larenz, so I know what I am offering is candy, baby, because not one told me flat out no like you and your establishment have. Even our homegirl Lisa seems to think it's a good idea."

JT looks at Larenz then Larenz says, "Is that right?"

Bill actually tries to swipe his face with the small napkin then just stops. "Oh, yeah, that's right."

"Lisa huh, tell me something?"

"What's good?"

"How long did you know she was down in Atlanta?"

Bill is matter of fact, "Lisa? Hell, I knew since the day she left. I told her to look you and Ania up. What, you didn't know?"

Larenz and JT lock eyes. "So, listen Bill, we thought about your offer and we think it's not a bad situation after all."

"You know, that's exactly what I said to Ania earlier this morning."

You can hear JT's chair scrape the wooden planks of the floor because he sits up so fast, but he remains in his chair.

"Ania?" Larenz wants to know.

"Yeah, I saw her this morning, going in to see Nicole."

"Nicole?" Larenz says.

"Yeah, man that's my homie. I mean it's like everybody from our hood done moved down to this piece. Me and Nicole stay in touch, since she's been down here too, I thought you knew that?"

"Nah, never knew."

"Yeah man, I mean facilities like the one she's been staying in ain't free, you know. When her people back home told me what was happening with her, I just couldn't let her go out like that, you know what I'm saying?"

"Yeah, yeah I do. So, listen we gotta' do this on a contract if we're going to do it."

Bill says, "It's the only way I do bid-ness, baby."

"I feel you, but it's important to understand that ever since I opened this club, I've tried to preserve the spoken word, R&B and jazz since day one. You of all people know how every got damn radio and media outlet that serves us, "us" meaning black folk, thinks the only thing we listen to is fuckin' rap music and all the "Baby's," no pun intended who actually perform it."

Bill says, "That's good L, I like your play on words. Always been a creative scribe."

Larenz says, "Nah, on soul, "Baby" he's my guy, we chop it up all the time."

"Good, I'll mention you to him, when we have dinner tonight."

"You do that. I'm serious though Bill, I'm not knocking what you do. But in a way, I am."

"Hold up L, what you mean?"

"I'm talking business our people and our communities peace. Look here, how many R&B and Jazz artist you got signed to your label?"

"I don't know, two maybe three."

"How many rappers?"

"Now, L, you ain't hear this from me, but you know they a dime a dozen. These new ones will rap for corn flakes nowadays. Matter fact most of them will pay me to put them on a record."

Larenz points out. "And the majority in my opinion, say nothing that is going to move us as a people forward."

"You're right, and I sign them, and get paid first. That's what I do."

"So, what I'm saying is, I don't want people down here thinking I done flipped my club bruh. I don't want rappers in here thinking I'm bowing down to their genre because your name is attached. It's not going to be like that. Now, you told me this group of yours has a nice little vibe to them, right?"

"Oh yeah, like I said, they are fluid man, and your club is the best fit for them it matches their content for sure."

"I'm just trying to keep my flow right. I like what I built here, it took years to build this up and we're the only people in Atlanta giving out this vibe and I want to keep it like that. So, every night, to make sure the essence of my club stays pure, before your people take the stage, all my poets, my jazz performers and R&B will bless the stage too and get to shine in front of the audience your new group is bringing in. It will give the audience a new perspective of music and creativity that has been long lost."

"No doubt, L. I can rock with that," Bill tells him.

"So, we have a deal?" Larenz and JT stand. Bill smiles. "Hold up now, that's not all, I'm tripling your offer."

Bill says, "I'm listening…?"

"I get all the proceeds times three," Larenz tells him.

Bill shakes his head and smiles some more. "Deal. I was prepared to give you four times the gate out my own pocket. Let's rock-this."

"Bet, let's go out to the bar and have a drink," Larenz suggests.

When they exit the office and go onto the main floor of the club, Kerry and Jill have just walked up on the stage. Jill is holding a microphone, and Kerry is standing strumming his bass, then sits down in his chair and looks back at his drummer and keyboardist. By this time, the new business partners are standing by the bar and Larenz is playing bartender because no one else is there to pour them their drinks as they look on to what's going on up on stage. It goes without saying that Kerry and Jill are killing it. Kerry is making his bass sing like he always does and Jill and her voice sound like heaven. When they are done everyone inside applauds.

Larenz hollers out and it echo's throughout. "Now, y'all know you are tough– ya dig."

"Sure the hell are," JT says and raises his glass.

Larenz turns to Bill. "Now, this is the type of act you need to be signing, they do this all day every day."

"Sure do," JT says.

Bill is amazed. "Oh, my goodness."

Jill hears them loud and clear and says, "Thanks guys, just up here getting some rehearsal time in. The acoustics in here are mad crazy. Love it, love it."

"And you did your thing as always," JT explains.

Kerry says, "Thanks bro, gotta' do what we do when we can do it."

Bill walks away from the bar a bit and closer to the stage. "So, who are you with now or are you doing it all independent these days, is what I want to know? Y'all not strangers to me. I know exactly who you are."

Jill is not shy about it. "We're talking to Viper records right now." Kerry gives her a look.

Bill punches out, "Oh, is that right? Well, you're talking to me, because I bought them about three weeks ago. You didn't know?" Bill is all the way up on stage now and daps Kerry up and hugs Jill. "Girl you can sang."

Kerry starts to play his guitar and his band members follow him softly as Jill and Bill chop it up.

Larenz and JT are at the bar, Larenz leans in and says, "Bruh, I've been thinking, and earlier today when ol'girl told me my son was dating her daughter that the two of us need to have a sit down. You know, make sure there's nothing else she's been hiding like another child or something."

"Word?" JT says, "After all these years?"

"Look man, I'm being honest; when I left Chicago with Ania it wasn't like the two of us weren't still, you know."

"Say less, that my brother is not a bad idea. Did you tell Ania yet that you ran into this old flame?"

"No need to yet. I really just need to find out if all other fronts are clear before I do that, not trying to run back and forth telling her this and that."

"You need me to ride you out?"

"No, I'll handle it. I'm going to call her, see if she'll meet me for coffee tomorrow morning then I will hit you up and we'll get back to business and get this contract ready for Bill to sign."

JT and Larenz look towards the stage. Bill is talking it up with Kerry and asks him if he could teach him how to play the bass the same way he does.

Home

The ladies are already wet from bringing in Nicole's first set of belongings, so they make up their minds to venture back outside to the car in the driveway to get more of her things. After the second go around, they decide to call it quits until the rain stops; the clouds are singing like they only do in Georgia.

"Girl…what's really going on?" Nicole wants to know.

"I know, right? It feels like we're in the tropics a damn rain forest or something. But you know I'm very partial to the rain because I'm sure I fell in love with Larenz for real standing in the rain with him one night," Ania remembers.

Nicole says, "I tell you what, if I had a man, I wouldn't have a problem going out there getting wet with him."

"Umm, sounds so good. Not giving one fuck," Ania snickers.

"Right. Give him some of this big girl." She laughs.

Ania says, "Girl, you are not big, you are nice and tight."

"Thank you, you're being too nice. I couldn't really workout like I wanted in there, spooky ass place. But now that I'm here I can get settled, get my discipline back in order and get myself the way I want to be." Nicole looks around. "Look at this, this is wonderful." They plop down on the couch and it's quiet for a few seconds. Almost like Nicole is trying to set her presence inside her new domicile and Ania just lets her have the time she needs. "Thank you so much Ania." Nicole smiles to keep from crying.

"Oh, girl you're welcome. I'm just so happy you're home."

"Thanks –it's so good to feel normal again."

Ania can feel Nicole about to tear up and she promised herself when Nicole got out of the facility she would always try her best to keep her smiling. Ania gets a burst of energy. "Hey, here look. Right over there is your computer and a cell phone. I already put you on my plan, so don't worry about anything. It's the new phone that everybody has, including myself. Everything you need is back here. The kitchen, dishes, stove, fridge, bathroom, bed with fresh linen. Girl you are good to go."

Nicole says, "You know when you told me, you and Larenz wanted me to stay with you guys, I cried and just cried."

"Aww honey," Ania consoles.

"But they were happy tears. I was so happy especially when they said I could leave and needed someplace to stay, and you stepped up like it wasn't even a thought."

"Because it wasn't. How long have we known each other?"

"Shoot… since pre-school. I remember we never talked in pre-school always would just stare at one another."

Ania smiles. "You remember that?"

"Sure do. Stare in line on recess. Stare at the lunch table. Stare in the hallways. Always had our eyes on each other."

"Wow, Nicole you have a hell of a memory."

"Then when you moved down here, with Larenz and left Chicago, I felt so alone. Even with my family in Chicago with me, things were not right. And what did I do?"

Ania laughs and hugs Nicole. "You called me and told me you were on the way."

"Sure, the hell did, and y'all were there for me then, too. Such good friends."

"Friends nothing, we're family and don't you ever forget it."

"Well fam', I need to ask you."

"What is it?"

"I heard you mention all the items waiting for me, did you happen to get me a Rose?"

Ania hesitates. "You know I thought about getting you some flowers but I thought they make you sneeze?"

"They do, you really do, know me don't you?"

"I try."

"But no– I'm talking the *Rose* toy." Ania doesn't have a clue and the look on her face lets Nicole know just that. "Gurl, for sexual frustration."

"Wait, what?" Ania laughs. "Rose toy—what the hell?"

"Same thing I said, but this lady who we called Mona, whose room was right next to mine, had one and I could hear her through those concrete walls enjoying herself all through the night, and I tell you, she would sleep all damn day long."

Ania laughs along with Nicole and says, "You could hear her through the concrete? C'mon, tell the truth, was Mona her real name?"

"I don't know, but that's what they called her."

"Well, baby I didn't get you one, but I'm sure we can go get it," Ania says.

"I'm telling you, it's been much too long for me, it's not like I had any pleasure up in that place. Hell, I was so scared in there that I didn't want to take my pants down to pee."

Ania says, "Okay, okay, let's go get you a Rose. If they're all that– I just might get me one too."

–

Right after the storm eases up. Ania and Nicole get back into the car, and journey to Starship, which would most likely have what Nicole wants, and they were in and out without a problem. The ladies returned to the guesthouse and are having so much fun talking about old times that Ania doesn't even realize Larenz was in the house until she walks into their bedroom. He is in the window looking down towards the guesthouse; all lit up. When Ania enters the room he turns around, holding a bottle of water, already in his lounging pants, t-shirt and slippers.

He says, "Hey, baby everything good? Nicole all set?"

"Yes, she's good. We got her moved in a bit and the next thing you know we are cooking breakfast for dinner and having a good time. I didn't even realize it was this late."

"That's good." He nods toward Ania. "What's in the bag?"

She looks down at it. "Oh, this? Just some lavender me and Nicole picked up for my bath. It's supposed to have a scent of rose, but we'll see."

"Cool, I'm glad you two are back together again."

"Me too, when they took her away and placed her in that facility Larenz I truly thought it was forever."

"And look at her now," Larenz says.

"GOD is so good," she confirms. "She is energetic, funny and ready to start her next chapter."

"I was planning on being here to welcome her home but things got a little busy down at the club; plus, we are a little short without Calvin. You know Kerry and Jill came through to get some work and they blessed the stage."

"They did? Aww, you should have told me."

"This was before the night time crowd baby, they just wanted to hear the sound get a little rehearsal in, you know they love the sound at the club. Then me and JT had to wrap up some business."

"So, how was your day otherwise?"

Larenz takes some of that water down from his bottle before he answers. "Out of control. You know we hired some consultants, they use to be city inspectors or something and they gave us a few items that might give us some problems down the line; so, we had to come up with a way to add some extra funds if we need them, so we don't have to dig into our own pockets."

"How?"

Larenz is now standing with his back facing Ania and he is removing his necklace and watch. At that point he remembers Bill mentioning that he saw Ania earlier in the day and he wants to see if she will acknowledge seeing him or not this time. He looks over his back a bit before he says, "Decided to go into a short-term business deal with Bill for a few weeks."

"That's a wonderful idea," she says. "It's always good to go into business with someone you know, when they bring the opportunity?"

Larenz turns around. "What do you mean?"

"Just that you've decided to go into business with him, it's a good thing—I don't know."

"I mean you're saying it like you already knew there was some business on the table?"

"No, no it's just that Nicole talks about him and all of the things he's doing so, I just naturally thought it was something like that." Ania walks towards the door in the bedroom. "I'm going downstairs for a bit, you need anything?"

"Wait, wait… let's talk about this for a minute."

Ania turns around. "Talk about what Larenz?"

"Let's talk about the reason you haven't told me you spoke to him? The reason why you didn't even let me know you saw him? Don't you think you should bring up that you've "run" into the person who almost shut us down for good because of the drama we went through?"

"What're you talking about, Larenz?"

"Why are you acting like you don't know what I'm talking about? Look here, he threw it up in my face the other night at the club. Yeah, that's right he told me you spoke to him then. You remember the night I spent in the guestroom? He also told me he saw you when you were going to see Nicole and you have said nothing about it."

"It's nothing to say, Larenz. I mean yeah, I saw him, we spoke—so what. After all the drama you and me been through you're acting like we still in our twenties running the streets of Chicago."

"No, I'm acting like I had to push some things out of my psyche to be with you, and the process wasn't easy; and why at this point in our lives; you, didn't want to bring it up?"

Ania tries to take in everything Larenz is throwing at her. "Look, there is no reason, so I'm gonna' ask you again do-you-want-anything-from-downstairs?"

"No, no I don't," Larenz tells her.

She walks towards the door, and looks at the bag in her hand. "Good, because I'm sleeping in the guest room tonight."

Early Chat

Early the next morning Larenz wakes up then gets ready for his day and feels no type of way about what he's getting ready to do. After the night and discussion with Ania, it doesn't sit too tough with him that he has to pull out of her that she did, in fact, see the man who came close to being the catalyst for the two not being an item; and Larenz feels some kind of way about it because of all of the work he has done within himself to even deal with the nonsense no matter how young they were. So, he gets through the morning without even seeing Ania before he leaves and now is in a coffee shop, sitting, stirring his coffee with a spoon looking down in his cup thinking about all that's on his mind and Lisa walks up to the table. "I hope you're not putting too much sugar in that drink?"

Larenz smiles and stands. "Hey, how are you, no sugar for me. Can I get you something?"

She says, "Whatever you're having please." Larenz holds his hand up and asks for another cup of java as they get comfortable at the table and it's really an awkward situation. Then out of the blue, Lisa says, "She's not your daughter, Larenz."

"Who, say what?"

"My daughter, whose dating your son."

"Whoa." Larenz is really surprised he thinks her admission is kind of hilarious. "Wait, so you think I would ask you that? It's so twisted. Just the thought turns my stomach."

She smiles and says, "I know right." Lisa can't stop smiling. "Just breaking the ice. Why are you so tense and things?"

"No, no I'm good. But quiet as it's kept, I was going to ask you did you have another besides your daughter that might be mine?" He gives Lisa a half smile then looks at his coffee.

"What?"

"Just saying, I was putting those years together and you never know."

"No, I don't"

"No?"

"No."

"Good."

"What?"

"I'm just saying."

"What're you just saying and why are you so tight up in the shoulders?"

"Who?"

"You..."

"I'm not tight?" Larenz moves his shoulders back and forth. "See, I'm good. You want me to get up and do some jumping jacks up in here or something, because I will."

"You are tight."

"This is just how I am. Remember we haven't seen each other in years, maybe I've changed a bit."

"Your ass ain't changed. Look at you. You're still the same weight and everything you might even weigh less than you did back in the day."

Larenz looks down at his body. "What?"

"Yes. Are you still eating all that fruit, drinking your water and no meat?"

"Yeah, I am. You look the same too."

She smiles and then says, "Thank you, but stop lying."

"No, seriously you do."

She says, "You too. Just tight that's all." She laughs. "So, tell me the real reason you wanted to see me?"

"Well, for one, I was wondering why, you never reached out when you came down?"

She doesn't answer right back. Thinks about her answer. "I thought about it. But we lead busy lives, plus I didn't want to get in the middle of anything. But I have read all your books, how many is it now?"

"I got quite a few, was hitting them hard for a minute but had to take a break and clear my mind a bit. I think my last one was my eighteenth, something like that. And I understand your reason for not reaching out."

In no time at all, their conversation strays off to everything they could think about over the span of years they had not been in contact with each other and without saying they are both surprised at how easy their conversation is moving along. It's almost like back in the day chatting it up nonstop, forgetting the time. They really have lost track of time catching up. They were over an hour in to it.

She says, "But, for real, for real, tell me the reason you wanted to see me? It's not wondering why I never contacted you since I have been here or any of that foolishness; c'mon keep it a buck with me."

Larenz looks up when he is alerted that her second cup of coffee is ready, and he tells Lisa to give him a second; he gets up and takes it off the countertop, and brings it over to her. Lisa has her eyes on him the entire time. "Here you go, nice and hot." She thanks him. "So, what were you saying?"

"You know what I was saying….tell me why you really wanted to see me?"

"I thought I already did? I mean seeing you, out of the blue was definitely a surprise, then you telling me your daughter is dating my son. I just wanted to be sure we didn't have anyone else connected to us, that I didn't know about because it's crazy out here and you never know until you really know." Lisa just stares at Larenz. "What? I'm being honest here."

"Are you really serious? Connected to us like a child?"

Larenz nods his head yes. "I mean I did leave quick, never called you again and didn't know how things were. So, yeah it has been on my mind, and if we did and I didn't know about it, it would all be on me. I would accept that because it wasn't right to leave the way that I did."

"Well, you're right. The way you left me was really hurtful. But no Larenz, the only thing you left me with, without saying goodbye was a broken heart. How's that?"

He puts his coffee down. "Good."

"What?"

"I mean, sorry I left, but good that I don't have a child that I've never met. I mean these kids go through so much nowadays. Plus, I don't know how I could explain that."

"Explain to who, your would-be child, or Ania?"

He pauses. "Both."

She says, "My intuition is saying Ania. I see you're still protecting her. You always did that, even when you weren't together."

"You're right. You're right, it's been like that."

"But I respect that you respect her in that way. Wish it could have been me. But anyway."

"Thank you, but here lately it seems that," Larenz notices the intrigue in Lisa's eyes as she sips her coffee and decides not to continue.

"No, please continue," she presses.

Larenz changes his thought about last night and gets upbeat. "No, it's okay. So, who would have ever thought my son, your daughter would be in a relationship? I mean, Jacob barely even speaks of who he is dating, but here lately, he has been given out hints, and to find out she's your daughter is quite a surprise."

"I know, right? When she told me his name and I heard that last name, Ways— I knew right away—he was yours."

"Yeah, it had to pique your interest. So, did you tell your daughter who I was and that you once upon a time were in a relationship with her man's daddy?"

"Relationship?"

"Yeah, you know."

"Uhh... we weren't really in a relationship the way I wanted because that's what you wanted."

"You're right."

"But no, I didn't tell her. I don't like bringing drama into her life. She finds out when she finds out. But I will tell her the clouded relationship part."

"Oh, that part?"

"Yes, that part. You know that was her that greeted you at the club?"

"Really? I thought she looked like you when I went back over the whole seeing you again moment. What's her name?"

"Zoe."

"Nice." Larenz takes a sip of his coffee.

Lisa says, "So, what did you think, I mean when you saw me again for the first time at my club?"

"Really?"

"Yes, what did you think?"

Larenz smiles. "I thought, I thought this really couldn't be real." Larenz picks up his coffee and smiles, and she smiles right back at him.

My Boy

If there is one person Larenz can go to and talk frankly about any subject besides JT it's his boy Isaiah. Isaiah still lives in Chicago with his wife and kids, who are at the age when they leave home; come back, and leave again, but he's cool with it because he knows how it is starting off, and he's just happy they're doing their own thing for the moment, and so the heck is he.

Isaiah answers the phone and goes right in on his boy. "My brother. You must not be listening to me when we chat. I specifically told your black ass—every day and that's every damn day between nine and ten in the morning, I'm getting a massage for the next year because my girl loves me like that and she hooked it up and I ain't wasting it. You got it?" Isaiah looks back at his masseuse, who is working his shoulders, and smiles after letting her know the pressure she is applying is just right.

Larenz is smiling on the other end. "Well, check this out black man. I forgot with your getting pampered ass. I need to talk."

Isaiah takes a deep breath. "Bout what?"

Larenz sings, "Lisa….."

Isaiah mocks him, "Leeesa….who is Leeesa…?"

"Lisa…..Lisa, nigga."

Isaiah says, "What? From the Cult Jam? What you doin' meeting her?"

Larenz tells him, "If you don't shut your old ass up, nah…nah… I'm talking about Lisa…Lisa you know…."

"Wait, you mean, little, big booty Lisa from our hood that you used to hit?"

"That's exactly who the fuck Lisa I'm talking about." Isaiah looks up and back at his masseuse and whispers that he needs a second. "Okay, you have my undivided attention."

"Dig, Jacob is turning twenty-five."

"I thought this was about little, big booty Lisa? Tell me something I don't know about my nephew."

"And I went to secure his spot at this club downtown called Marbles."

"Okay."

"When I asked to speak to the owner or whatever, guess who comes out of nowhere?"

"Do you really want me to guess?"

"Messed my head up instantly bruh, I thought I was dreaming or in another world."

Isaiah takes another deep breath and slows down the pace. "Okay, listen up. Just let me put this out there right now, if Ania finds out… she's whipping your muthafuckn' ass, no questions asked."

"Nobody's worried about that, right now. I can handle that."

"What? What're you talking about?"

"Check this out. Your boy Bill is down here and she on numerous occasions has conveniently not mentioned to me that she has seen him or talked to him."

"Wait, wait wait, wait wait. Brother, I am too old to hear some doo-doo about, Bill and his pinhead ass."

"Well, that's what it is. And I'm feeling some kind of way about it because if she can't tell me that simple situation, I'm beginning to question why? Plus, I just went into a business deal with his ass."

Isaiah can't believe he needs to take one more deep breath to keep his zen intact. "You-did-what?"

"Had to bruh, tell you later about it."

"Look, just make sure JT stays close aight? One thing you don't want is some on-going beef with Bills stupid ass. And don't forget your ass is married and at some point you got to talk and work things out. Don't sit back and worry about it though, tighten up your belt and find out what's up with her silence."

"You're right. You're right. But dig—I have something else to tell you."

"Hurry up, I'm on the clock, what is it?"

"Lisa has a daughter and she's dating Jacob."

Isaiah whispers into the phone but he is forceful. "Black man, I'm telling you this situation ain't going to end well. Tell Ania as soon as you can and don't say another word to Lisa until you do, you got that?"

"Yeah man, I got it."

"Bet, now let me get back to it."

Let's Eat

Jacob and Zoe are strolling through Ponce City Market. They sit down and look around. "Look, I don't care what we eat baby," Jacob says. "But I'm hungry so, you just choose."

Zoe examines their surroundings then realizes. "Don't you know this will be one of your last meals before you turn the big two-five tomorrow? I want it to be delicious, so we can have long lasting memories." Jacob places his hand on his stomach.

"Okay, cool, choose something so that my stomach can remember."

Zoe pats him on his leg a few times. "But wait, wait how do you feel?"

He says, "I'm good. I mean it doesn't feel any different you know? I remember when I was younger I would always say, damn I can't wait until I'm twenty-one, then that came nothing special, twenty-two, it was just as blah, after twenty-three I swear to you I was like this needs to slow down a bit 'cause I got things I need to do and it's moving so fast."

"Facts, it is going by at a rapid pace, but I want you to really enjoy this one, okay, baby?"

"No doubt, I will. We're going to turn up for sure." They agree, then start talking about how much they're going to drink and how they already know how certain friends of theirs are going to act out like they always do. Jacob looks at an older couple pushing a stroller and they look happy as can be looking at their child inside the stroller. "Damn now that I'm turning the big two-five, I probably should be getting ready for that part of my life too," he says and nods at the proud couple.

It's like Zoe sings, "What…You…?"

"What do you mean by that? Out here sounding like an Ella Mai new single. I'm serious."

"Because it's a shock to me. Mr. Fashion and business sense out here, thinking about a kid?"

"Hell yeah. I mean, gotta' start thinking about it sometime; just think, if I wait too much longer, I'll be the old dad at the games and I ain't trying to do that. Or especially at the school functions and field days. I need to walk up in there with the nice fit and my body right to represent for my kid, you know?"

She pauses. "Well, you need a female to help you do that–don't you?"

"Hell yeah, I do."

"Well, you better find her and vet her to make sure you two are a match."

He smiles. "What do you think I've been doin'?"

"Really, I don't know, so you tell me?"

Jacob looks around he doesn't like where they are sitting and grabs his girl by her hand. "Come on let's move." It's not like they move a few feet away. They start to walk towards an elevator and when it's about to close they rush inside. Zoe doesn't say a word and when the elevator reaches the top they get off on the rooftop of Ponce and find a seat where there is a perfect view.

"Wow, this is nice. How'd you know I wanted to come up here?" Zoe says.

"I didn't, I just made a decision for us plus, where we were sitting wasn't right for us. It didn't feel right."

"Right for what?"

"Right enough to ask you to marry me, that's what." Jacob pulls out a ring and pops the question. Zoe is so surprised that she can't even say yes or no.

Unexpected

The next night. Larenz and Ania are together with friends at Nickels for the planned celebration of Nicole being home, having a son turning twenty-five, and kicking off the business venture with Bills new act. They are sitting at their table with JT, Nicole and Bill. Ania is partially vexed, looking side-eyed at Larenz; she is somewhat impressed with him for inviting Bill to join them at their table but she knows Larenz and the conversations they've had concerning Bill that he is just keeping him close.

JT looks around at the table. "So… mom and dad how does it feel, that your son is a whole grown ass man now?"

Larenz has his chest puffed out with pride. "Oh yeah, he's been a man for sometime now but you're right, he's a full-grown ass man now baby."

JT points out, "This is true, but I know you remember when that twenty-five hit, it's a different ball game, unless you can't remember that far back."

Ania jumps right in, "Oh, yes he remembers because I always have to hear about the stories of how he and Isaiah use to run the streets back in Chicago." Bill, Nicole and Ania all agree then reminisce a bit.

"Look bruh, it feels good ya dig? We been blessed not to have him get into any trouble, because you know how they're locking them up. Then to graduate college a few years ago, at this point, we good."

Nicole hasn't said much yet, but the smile on her face is showing everyone that she is getting comfortable being out. She adds, "Pretty soon, it will be some little ones running around on that stage over there."

Ania beams with joy. "Oh, girl that would be so nice."

Then JT gets messy. "And, maybe he'll have two wives to watch the kids."

Nicole says, "Say what now?"

Ania pushes her back into her seat and says, "Nuh-uh… JT?"

Everyone at the table looks in JT's direction and wonders where the heck he is going with all this. In fact, Ania has to take a sip of her drink. JT fills them in, "Believe me when I tell you. Constructing a tribe is the way to go nowadays. Straight up making villages and kinship to survive to flourish in today's society."

Larenz sets down his drink. "Negro, what're you talking about?"

"Obviously, y'all been watching too much cable and have authentic life jumbled with those made to order storylines because I'm talking some real-world circumstances right now," JT tells them. They are all looking at him without a clue. "Okay, let me get y'all up on game since the idea is so damn brand new to you. Well, you know I have a little something over across town, right?"

Larenz says, "Yeah, we know. More than we want to know."

"Anyway, we were sitting down talking and she is telling me that a girlfriend of hers, who from time to time goes out with my girl, you know…when I'm out here handling business."

Larenz picks up his drink, smiles and says, "Watch out now."

Ania tells him, "Stop," then looks at Larenz as though he better not get any ideas.

JT can't wait to tell it. "So, the friend says, she likes the way I move and she wants to know if I would be willing to be head of a tribe situation where there is just the three of us making things happen in our own little circle."

"Oh, my goodness—have I been gone that long?" Nicole says.

Larenz gets in it next, "Hold up, hold up. I want to know

what you said. That's what I want to know?" Nicole co-signs.

JT inquires, "You really want to know?" They are all sitting looking at JT waiting for his answer. He grins. "So, now they calling me big-daddy. I'm leaning on going that way."

Larenz can't hold back, "Right…..foolish daddy, that's what they're calling your ass."

Nicole gives Larenz some dap then says, "You mean sucker for a daddy."

As they go in on JT and he defends himself. Bill looks at his watch, tells everyone he'll be right back then gets up from the table and walks toward the stage. The lights dim in the club on cue and Bill steps up on the stage and everyone begins to quiet down.

Bill doesn't hesitate there is no confusion that he is in his element. "Good evening, I'm Bill Cash, the founder of Vindictive Entertainment and with the help of my friends, Larenz and Ania Ways, who we all know and love." There is applause from the crowd. "That's right give it up. I'm honored and humbled to announce that for the next four weeks, we will be headlining my new act Chit-Chat, to get the pulse of Atlanta because everyone knows this is where it starts for many, and I wanted you to see them first. We appreciate you being here." Larenz and JT are very focused in on what he is saying because Bill never went over with them what he would be mentioning to their guests. He says, "I'm also so happy to announce that I have a verbal agreement to sign these two wonderful musicians that you all know so very well, Kerry and Jill." The audience applauds and the lights come up on stage and Bill walks off as Kerry and Jill kill a song. When they are finished it's like magic and Bill walks back to the table and sits down. He says, "Oh, my goodness. Did you hear that? That's why I'm signing them on the dotted line."

Ania mentions, "Oh, they sound so good."

Nicole adds, "I can't wait to give them a hug."

Everyone is recovering from the performance at the table and Bill says, "So everybody good?" Larenz is looking at Bill stumped now because when he got up from the table the first time he was sitting next to Nicole now he is sitting next to Ania.

Larenz says, "Yeah, we good. So, you signed Kerry and Jill?"

"Yeah, we started to chit-chat a bit, no pun intended and got a little verbal agreement so far and we're talking things out."

Larenz says, "You know they're my people, got to give them everything they want."

"Gotdamn right. I will and I am. I will give them the store so we can get paid baby. They will definitely eat with me." Everyone at the table is in agreement and happy for Kerry and Jill. Then Bill starts in, "Okay now, let's hear some more about that tribal situation? Is that still on the table for discussion because, for some, it's a win-win?"

Nicole says, "Yeah, JT finish talking about these women out here looking for a tribal hookup. I mean, I'm open to learning that is the least I can do."

"So, I didn't know Atlanta is so diversified; Just sayin', I knew The A was poppin', but not poppin' like that." Bill comments.

Larenz lets him know, "Not everywhere in The A as you call it."

Bill concedes. "True that, true that." Bill gives a quick look at Ania. "Well, I've been all over the world and it ain't nothing new to me. From coast to coast, city to city, it's going down. I mean somebody sees someone they like, and feels there's an opportunity to make a situation better so grown people make a decision to enhance what is. I'm all about enhancement myself."

JT is in quick, "Well, I don't know if I'm trying to go in full scale enhancing at the moment. I need to see if they running game. If not, I might get with it and go in at a hundred percent watching my back every step of the way."

Bill points at JT then says, "Smart man."

Ania adds, "Yeah you wait a little bit JT. We don't want to see you out here ass out in the streets, looking for your car and money."

Everyone laughs and chimes in then Bill says to Nicole, "So, Nicole are you enjoying yourself, mi amor?"

"Yes, Bill I am, thank you, very much. It's so good to see everyone. This is really wonderful. I mean the conversation is a little different, we used to sit around and talk about who had the best voice, Tina Marie or Whitney and now y'all out here talking about taking care of tribes and things."

Ania lets her know, "We're happy to see you too. And our Whitney, Tina debate is still ongoing girlfriend." Then there are some comments all around the table about which singer they like the most then Ania says, "Let's see, Nicole the only person you haven't seen yet is…." And on cue Jacob walks up hand in hand with Zoe and gives and gets huge hugs from everyone. "Jacob I was just mentioning you!" Ania tells him.

"Hey mom, pops everybody."

Larenz wants to know, "What're you doing here bruh? You're supposed to be at your birthday party."

"Now you know I had to step out for a second, say hello and thanks for the setup– it's lit up in there."

Bill interjects, "Wait, wait a minute, so you left your own birthday party, to come say thanks to your parents?" Jacob looks at Bill and wonders who the hell he is.

Larenz picks up on his confusion and says, "Son, this is Bill."

Bill stands and reaches out his hand. "Nice to meet you Jacob. I've known your father since forever all the way back to Chicago and we are business partners for about a month or so."

Jacob looks at his father because most of the time Larenz runs ideas past him but he is clueless about their dealings. He says, "Nice to meet you and yes, I needed to say thank you before the night was over."

Bill says, "Now see, if I had a son I would want him to be just like yours. I can see right now, you two did a good job with him and look at him… he's way better looking than his daddy too."

Larenz brushes past Bill's comment. "Son are you going

to introduce us to your lady friend?" Larenz can clearly see her mother, Lisa now all through Zoe.

"Jacob smiles everybody this is Zoe, she's my…."

Zoe cuts him off when she faintly recognizes Larenz then she looks over at JT and he waves at her and she definitely recognizes him because she served him a drink at Marbles. At the same time, Larenz makes room for them at the table and tells them to sit down. Zoe says, "Hello everyone, but actually I was on my way to the ladies room I'll be right back." As she walks away she can hear Ania mention how pretty she is.

Larenz gives Jacob some dap then says, "Son let's walk over to the other side for a moment I need to talk to you for a quick second."

"Pops, we're just here for a second bruh, I just wanted to say thanks and I was going to dip." Larenz smiles and lets everyone know he'll be right back and he and Jacob walk away to the other side of the club.

As soon as they are away from the table Jacob says, "What's up pops?"

Larenz gathers himself. "Look here son, there's something you should know."

Jacob smiles. "No, no let me go first."

"Aight, cool what is it?"

"I got engaged to Zoe." Jacob is smiling ear to ear. It's the first time he actually let his pops in on his personal business since his prom date and he is sincerely happy about it.

"Say what?"

"Yeah man, we got engaged."

"Engaged?"

"Yup she's the one…"

"Jacob I wish you would have come to me…." Then they are interrupted by taps on a snare drum in the club which signals someone in the club wants to bless the guests with a poem. The lights go down and a spotlight appears down below and now it's much too quiet for Larenz and Jacob to continue their conversation so their eyes focus on the upcoming performance. Everyone back at the table is looking on as well, ready for the poem that is soon to be delivered.

When the performer gets in position in the middle of the spotlight Jacob mumbles, "That's Zoe's mom?"

Larenz can't believe it and mumbles, "And your mother is about to lose her mind."

"That's Zoe's mom, pop," Jacob says again.

Larenz shakes his head. "Yeah, I know."

Zoe walks out of the hallway from the restroom and looks on stage and realizes her mother is about to perform and is confused as anybody. Jill and Kerry have now joined the table with everyone. Nicole, Ania and Bill.

Nicole shades her eyes from the spotlight down on the stage and says, "I wasn't sure at first, but that's Lisa from back home; then she looks at Ania, who has stiffened and seems to have an infrared light beaming from her eyes zooming right towards Lisa.

Ania takes a closer look and mumbles, "This bitch."

Bill takes it all in with a crooked smile on his face as everyone has their eyes on the stage as Lisa begins to read her poem right after she clears her throat.

"Just to let you know this is my birthday
I have something that I want to say.
I used to have a smile on my face
but it was a long, long time ago,
when I couldn't wait to see his face.
That's when I was a young lady though.
Can you believe we recently again touched
eyes; I couldn't believe I still had butterflies.
Our conversation wasn't half bad either
made me remember when we'd talk on the
phone I wouldn't dare lay down the receiver.
But it was such a long time ago
and I truly felt I let all those feelings go.
I guess it's true what they say
real true feelings never ever go away.
As he spoke to me I watched his lips
it wasn't difficult to imagine his kiss.
I had so many thoughts running through my mind
really thought they had disappeared with all the
years that were left behind.
I have no regrets of what I said tonight.
Remember it's my birthday, if I'm lucky I'll be
granted a present and will dream of what we use to have
all through the night."

Lisa thanks the crowd for listening then walks off stage. Larenz takes a quick look over at the table, and he can feel Ania's infrared light burning like hot coals right through his ass. Jacob looks at his father and says, "Wow, who knew she had bars?"

Larenz is numb standing, shaking his head with his hands in his pockets, knowing he has himself a situation. Jacob looks up and can see Zoe go after her mom as she is walking toward the door. Larenz pushes, "Look son, that's what I wanted to talk to you about." Jacob is still observing Zoe and Larenz presses even more to talk to him. "Jacob, look; I need to tell you something." Jacob finally tunes in to Larenz. "Look, Zoe's mom and I used to have this thing back in the day."

Jacob is staggered with squinted eyes. "Yo', leave the jokes for when we're in the kitchen chilling."

"It's not a joke, I'm serious. I dated her and your mother around the same time. But it was a long time ago. Back in Chicago."

Jacob is dazed by his words. "What?"

"I'm being serious here. I mean we were young. You know how it is when you're trying to find your way. It's something you should know and I swear to GOD I didn't know she was in Atlanta until I went to book your party at her club."

"So, what is she doing here pops? And that poem, what was that? Was that about you? Oh, wow I need to find Zoe." Jacob walks away in a rush.

Music is now playing in the club. Larenz takes a deep breath and before he can exhale Ania is in his face. Bill and everyone else at the table are looking across the club at them wondering what is going on. But JT knows and is just moving his head left to right as he looks down at his drink. When Bill asks JT what is going on, JT tells him to mind his business.

Ania goes right in and says, "Oh, oh, oh, I mean, really Larenz? I mean, would you mind telling me what that was all about? A freakn' poem?"

Larenz is looking around the club trying to ensure they are not the center of attention and he tries to smile. He doesn't know it, but Bill is smiling too. Larenz feels like the damn stage spotlight is on him for all to see. "Look baby, it's not what you think."

"Oh really, butterflies, eyes, feelings– what the fuck do you mean it's not what I think? Then what is it, huh? And don't stand here and tell me what I'm thinking."

Larenz looks around, "No, I'm just saying I didn't know she was going to come here and do that."

Ania says, "Well you need to tell me something and you can start with your freakin' conversations…..conversations Larenz?"

"Ania, baby calm down, we're in the club. Look, I didn't know she was going to show up here. I mean, I knew she was here."

"What do you mean, you knew?"

"Like I said, I knew she was here, in Atlanta. Look let's go outside for a minute so we can talk." Larenz tries to grab her hand, Ania resists and walks in front of him out of the club to go get her explanation of what the hell is going on.

Chaos

Jacob finally catches up to Zoe and he kisses her on the cheek and then he wants to know if she's okay.

"Jacob did you see that? That was my mother up on that stage." Zoe's eyes are getting moist and she truly doesn't know what is going on.

"Yes, baby I saw her," Jacob tells her. "Who knew?"

They start walking then Zoe stops. "Wait seriously, what was that? What is she even doing here?"

Jacob takes his keys out of his pocket and says, "Look, we need to go, there's something I need to tell you."

She looks at him sternly. "Like what?"

He takes off walking again then looks at her. "It really doesn't have anything to do with us. It's our parents on some Love Jones shit."

Zoe stops again. "Would you wait a minute? What're you talking about?"

"C'mon let's go." Jacob takes her hand and they are headed toward the door; walking so fast they don't even notice Larenz and Ania standing outside a few feet from the entrance. Larenz notices and reaches out for them and tells Zoe it was nice to meet her and for the two to be careful but they don't hear him. They hop in the car and they drive out the parking lot.

–

Ania is standing in front of Larenz and waiting for her gotdamn explanation of events. Larenz is like, "Baby, c'mon now, don't give me that hands on hip stance out here in public. You know we don't even get down like that." Ania doesn't move right away, and they are at a stand-still; then, she puts her arms down.

She says, "Look, I really don't know how you want me to stand. Should I put my arms all around you like I want to take you home and make love to you– like I've been trying to do since forever and act like we don't have any problems right now, or what? Because didn't I just hear another bitch tell the entire city of Atlanta that she is feeling my man?"

Larenz's mind is telling him he should have listened to

Isaiah and JT because at the moment he doesn't know what to say; the entire situation has his head spinning and he is lost for words which never happens.

–

But Jacob is full of words as he drives back to his party with Zoe.

He utters, "Whew, this is crazy let's just get back to my party and have some drinks."

Zoe is looking out at the Atlanta skyline through the darkness and replies, "Jacob what is going on? Do you know?"

"All I know is my pops just told me, he and your mom, used to get together."

She turns to him. "Wait, what? Jacob what? What're you talking about?"

He reaches for her hand and they embrace together tighter than ever before. "Babe I don't know. That's all I got. Him just saying something about how they were young and he didn't know your mom was even in Atlanta until he booked my party."

"Well, I didn't even know that was your dad until tonight but I remembered him when he came into the club-that's why I excused myself when you introduced us. Just wait until I talk to her. Why didn't she tell me that was your father? And that poem? What would make her go and do that? Not only is this your birthday, it's hers too. Did she say on that stage that she still remembers the dick?"

Jacob looks over at her and the car swerves a bit. His

face is twisted, voice a pitch higher and anxiety growing by the second. "What? When did you hear that? What were you listening too? I think she said lips or something like that. You need to relax some; I didn't hear a word about some dick."

"You're right, you're right. No that's not what she said, I can't even remember it was so embarrassing."

Jacob pushes on the gas to go a little faster then smirks when he realizes. "Damn, my pops use to smash your mom."

Zoe pushes back. "You don't have to say it like that."

"Well, that's how it is."

She pushes back again. "Well, maybe she just use to smash your dad. You ever think about that?" Silence takes over the car giving them both time to think then they turn to each other. Zoe says, "Wait, how long ago was this?"

Jacob understands her reasoning without saying, "Oh, hell no. We couldn't be. We better not be?"

Zoe tells him, "Freakin' drive this car, Jacob I need to talk to my mother."

He makes the car go faster and says, "We both do, are you crying? Zoe stop crying." Then they both release their hands at just the thought.

–

Larenz and Ania are still standing outside the club together.

Ania says, "I want to be clear. So, she's been here all this time and you never knew?"

"Exactly, what I'm saying," Larenz lets her know.

"But you found out not long ago, and still didn't tell me?"

Larenz pauses. "Wait Ania, we're not doing it like that, okay. You have run into Bill two times and didn't tell me anything at all about it."

"What?"

"That's right, so I didn't really think it mattered me telling you about her. I mean it use to, but maybe it doesn't anymore."

Ania is taken back by his words she just seems to have a flashback of all the years they have shared together and shc stares Larenz down and the heat fuming from her eyes have instantly turned into tears. She tries a few times but Ania is unable to speak, she puts her head down and walks toward the entrance of the club as Larenz somewhat throws his hands in the air and calls after her, but she doesn't respond.

–

Meanwhile, Bill is inside Nickels and he is using the night and the crowd to his advantage to hype his new act again. He almost has overstayed his welcome by running his mouth so much then he finally introduces his group for a second set and makes way so they can perform in front of the anxious audience. JT sees Ania walk in then back towards the table and then Larenz shortly after.

JT walks up to Larenz, "Yo, what-is-goin'-on?"

"Heck if I know, but I need to find out. Man, did you hear Lisa?"

"I heard her, everybody did. Bruh, when you told me, you two had something going on, I was like okay whatever. But that sounded like you had everything going on and she hasn't forgot about it one little bit."

"Forget that, it wasn't even like that." Larenz looks at the act on stage and the type of crowd this new act has drawn to his establishment combined with what he has going on at the moment, it is quickly taking him out his element of cool, calm and collective. For the first time ever, he has a hip-hop crowd stomping, twerking and grinding on his flawless black marble dance floor and the weed flowing through is as thick as it's ever been. "Damn, I gotta' put up with this for a month? We gotta' make sure we watch the count up in here; I don't want the fire department pulling up."

JT tells him, "Stay focused, look around we're making much bread. If it stays like this we're gonna' make out real nice."

Larenz gives his words some thought then walks back over to the table and he and JT sit down with everyone else. Ania is now sitting next to Nicole and everyone at the table is unruffled but concerned without a word. Almost like they are waiting on an explanation of Lisa's poem but it damn sure isn't coming from Larenz because he is just as bewildered as anybody. They sit and listen to the group on stage and JT is having a small conversation with Nicole and Larenz leans in to talk to Ania.

"Ania look, we can talk about this at home okay? I mean really, I didn't know that was going to happen and I truly apologize for it, but not because it's true, but because it happened and embarrassed you. Hell, both of us." Ania doesn't respond she is just looking throughout the club in a non-caring fashion. Bill is standing across the club and Larenz notices Ania looking in his direction. "Something over there interesting?"

"Something like what?"

"Whatever you're looking at?"

"Do you even know what I'm looking at?"

"I know what it looks like you're looking at."

"Well, if you know, you know and if you don't you don't." She turns and looks Larenz directly in his eyes. "Is this what you want? My eyes completely on you? Thought you would be tired of that since everyone at this table has been looking at you since your friend read her little poem."

"Look, Ania it's not like that."

"Is that right?"

"Yeah, it's right."

"Well, maybe we both need to go home because we're seeing things up in here." Ania stands up and asks Nicole if she is ready, and Larenz whispers to JT if he would take them home to which he agrees.

–

Larenz has been through enough already and it's evident that what he and Ania have going on will not be solved and he is pissed about the entire situation. He is not ready to go home just yet. He really wants to know what was on Lisa's mind coming to the club and doing her poem. But first he needs to sit down in his office to get his bearings. As soon as he has finally had the chance to take a deep breath there is a knock at the door.

"Calvin? What's up? I thought you were having fun in the sun?"

Calvin steps all the way into his office and shuts the door behind him drowning out most of the sound coming from the club. "Yeah, me too, but I never made it." Larenz now has more muddle on top of his confusion. "Look the money you gave me, I went to the bank cashed the check went home to pack and when it was time to go to the airport to get out of here, the money was gone and so was Cam."

Larenz is drained. "What and the hell is going on?"

"I really don't know. When I look and talk to Cam it's like I don't even know him right now."

Larenz thinks about it and gets up to open the safe. "Look, you know what. Forget that, I still want you to go."

"No, no, no Larenz. You already did that. I need to get a handle on what the hell is going on with him. Kris is worried sick over Cam and there is no way she is leaving to go anyplace right now." Larenz tells him he understands. Calvin says, "Look, the only thing for me to do is go home and sit and worry, but I'm not going to do that. I'm going back on the job help with the close and anything else."

"Sure man, yeah. Glad you're back, if you need anything let me know." Calvin walks back out to the club and Larenz just sits at his desk and thinks about how quickly all this drama in his life has unfolded.

Tell Us

Jacob is pushing his car at a nice rhythm now and the raspy dual exhaust on his Hellcat is humming like a mother. He is making it through every single traffic light he approaches with the windows rolled down and sunroof wide open taking in all the fresh air he can to maintain his composure; with Post Malone and "Rockstar" on blast. He and Zoe have not said much more other than wondering if Lisa would be at the club or not so they can talk to her.

So much is running through their minds; for one how could such an exciting birthday weekend turn into drama and trauma in just a few hours. When he proposed to Zoe, and when she accepted, there was no way they thought that in a matter of hours, they would be worried about if they might need to send their DNA to AfricanAncestory.com. From time to time, while Jacob is driving, he looks over at Zoe to see if there is the slightest of resemblance, and she does the same thing, and every time she does, she holds onto her stomach because she feels like she is going to become sick. She is pissed that this is happening to her and at the same time this is the first time they have witnessed one another go through some real-life adversity and it is quite different from the reality they know about one another after almost an entire year of dating. Zoe is erratic and jumpy and has damn good reason to be. Jacob is reserved, quiet and upset. He is slapping himself because in his mind he is the one to blame. His first thought is that he should have talked more about Zoe to his parents so that maybe during one of those conversations they always have in the kitchen in the morning during some breakfast, that if he mentioned Zoe or her mother, it would have sparked some intrigue, and questions as to who he really was dating in the first place. He promises to himself that he will let them in more, and he feels like a fool because he has just proposed, and it looks like it can blow up in his face.

When they finally reach the parking lot of the club. Jacob pulls up to the front door and stops his car and they get out.

Normally he opens the door for Zoe and usually she doesn't move until he does because this is just what they did. He always respected his queen that way. But this time he forgets and Zoe doesn't care about the door. She hops out the car damn near faster than he does because she wants to talk to her mother and she is hoping like hell she is back in her office so they can do so. They walk right through Jacob's lit ass party and Zoe doesn't even knock on the office door; Jacob is behind her and once inside, they notice Lisa sitting behind her desk pouring herself a drink.

Lisa looks up and smiles. "Hey you two. Enjoying the party? You really have some nice friends Jacob." She sits her bottle down and takes whatever she is having straight to the head.

Zoe runs her hand through her hair takes a deep breath then says, "Mom, what's going on?"

Lisa says, "What do you mean?"

Zoe is direct. "No, that's not what we're doing–okay? Don't do it." Jacob and Zoe are standing side by side and they look at one another and take a few steps away from each other because their heads are really tangled and clouded. "I'm talking about that poem, you did at Nickels, what is going on?" Lisa reaches for the bottle and pours herself another drink. She takes it straight down and looks at them. "Look is Jacob my brother or what?"

Jacob stiffens his body waiting for an answer then says, "We need to know Lisa."

It's like Lisa is waiting for the burn to subside in her throat from her drink. She struggles to say, "Hell no. He is not your brother."

"So, he is not my brother?"

"Girl no." Jacob and Zoe turn and look at one another and smile.

Jacob says, "Whew. Baby whew." They start to hug and then begin to look each other over as if they are checking for injuries after an accident or something.

Lisa is confused, "What the hell are you two doing?"

Zoe turns and looks at Lisa. "We are getting married, that's what we're doing and this is my man and going to be your son-in-law."

Lisa is lost for words but she stands up. "Baby, congrats come here and hug your mother." Zoe does and Jacob is all smiles. "Come here Jacob," Lisa says and she gives him a hug too. "This is such a surprise."

They let go of Lisa and grab each other again this time Zoe lets out a scream and kisses Jacob all over his face. "I'm so sorry baby. I'm so sorry."

He lets go of her. "Sorry for what baby? We're good."

"I'm just so sorry for being mad at you for not knowing if we really were or not, that's all."

"Wait, so, you were putting that all on me?"

She smiles. "Yes, I'm so sorry."

He laughs. "It's okay, I'll take the smoke for you baby. Hey, c'mon let's go turn up and enjoy this party." Jacob walks over to Lisa's desk takes her bottle of which he now sees is tequila, opens it up and takes a heavy swig then sits it back down on her desk then tells Lisa it's okay because they are family now.

"Okay, but let me talk to mom, for a minute and I will be out," Zoe tells him. Jacob gives her another kiss and a hug and is out the door. When he leaves Lisa walks back and sits down behind her desk and Zoe is standing with her hands on her hips. Lisa looks at her and Zoe gives it right back to her. "Okay, is there something going on with you that I don't know about?"

"No, I'm fine. Just fine." Lisa reaches for her bottle and pours another.

"No, you're not. You walk into a club and spill your guts with a poem in front of hundreds of people you don't even know. That to me is not fine."

"Well, daughter of mine, it needed doing."

"Well, I don't understand, but let me tell you what I do understand and I'm getting it all second hand. Not from you. So, you and Jacob's dad use to be together, and you go to his club in front of all his friends, family, and clientele and tell everyone about it, in a poem? Not to mention, me. Who does that?"

"Those were not my intentions; I didn't even know you were there."

"But you did, and I was."

"Look, here's the deal."

"Yes, please tell me. Please explain."

"When you're with a person that you care about."

"Let me stop you mama, you're talking over twenty-years ago, right?"

"Right. So, stop interrupting and hear me out." Zoe sits down in a chair on the other side of the desk, folds her arms and tunes in. "As I was saying, when you're with a person that you care about. And everything is done by that person that makes you feel like they genuinely care for you too. Then that person ups and leaves without a word with someone else, and you hear on the street, that the person you cared about so deeply walks around and swears that what you two had together meant absolutely nothing. Just something to pass the time, I tell you right now as a person who loves and cares for others deeply, you will never get over it, never—no matter how long it's been because, pain is pain." Lisa is planning on drinking the entire bottle and forgetting about her night, so she picks up her bottle again to pour another. Zoe stands up and snatches the bottle away.

"No mom. You're better than this. All this drinking. Okay, I get it, Jacobs dad was someone who was special to you. But holding onto something for over twenty-years, is a bit much in my opinion."

"Because you're young and these are different times. Your generation doesn't even have a memory bank in your brains."

"Wow, mom, really?"

"Right. Now, give me my bottle back and go party with your man."

Ride Home

All JT can do during the journey to drop Ania and Nicole off is listen to them as they chat it up in the backseat with his eyes constantly moving from the road to his rearview mirror, engaging the ladies.

"I mean really, what a hapless night for all to see," Ania says.

Nicole is soothing, "It's not that bad, really."

Ania turns her shoulders towards Nicole, even lifting off the seat a bit. "I'm so glad you're my friend Nicole and you're trying to protect me, but really, it is– that bad."

Nicole pushes her body close to the front of the Range Rover. "It's okay, won't everything be okay JT?"

JT looks into the back quickly and can see Ania is texting. "Yeah, yeah, what would life be without a little drama? It's nothing that a conversation won't fix."

Nicole points to JT and says, "Exactly."

Ania looks up from her phone. "Well, I'm glad y'all think so, 'cause I think it stinks to the core. I mean Lisa? Lisa? Lisa? Messy ass Lisa, is living here and has been all these years, and Larenz didn't know?"

JT shakes his head and says, "I ain't getting in y'all's business."

Ania says, "Negro, what? Well, you are all in our business and have been for years." Then she laughs off her comment.

"I-am-not. Don't believe this Nicole." JT smiles.

"JT can you honestly say to me, you're not in our business? You stay in our business man, admit it."

JT thinks on it. "Okay, I guess you're right. But I was there when he first saw this Lisa. I mean, I don't know her, but I can honestly say when Larenz saw her, he was in disbelief. He couldn't believe it, matter of fact he was kind of pissed."

Ania says, "About what?"

"He was just wondering, you know. Wondering what she was doing here, almost like someone has been here all these years watching him and he never knew."

Nicole chimes in, "I can understand that, because when I was in that damn facility, I hated the feeling of knowing someone was watching me, but I couldn't really tell who it was."

Ania just finishes texting. "Well, I don't know. This is all too much right now."

After a non-stop convo, JT finally gets them home safe and walks Ania inside, and Nicole thanks him and goes to the guesthouse. "Ania you good?"

"Yes, thank you so much JT."

JT turns to the door then stops. "You know I hate to see you and L go through it. I mean we talk about things all the time."

Ania smiles a bit. "Yeah, like what?"

JT teases her and smiles back. "Well… you know I can't tell you exactly, because that would definitely be breaking our bro code."

"Oh, is that what it is?"

"Exactly, we're just like that. We got years into this and I can tell you. All he does is talk about you. He's not sneaking around, he's not out here flirting. Shoot, I have to be honest, I never even seen the nigga look at another woman."

"JT, if you don't shut up. Never? Don't play me."

He smiles. "No, I'm dead ass. I mean when we were coming up I used to tease him all the time about being so young and tied down."

"Tied down? That's what he was?"

"You know what I mean, married. Back in the day when we were just getting started being married was the furthest from anyone's mind. Then to hang around a cat that young who already had someone he wanted to be with for the rest of his life was rare when we were coming up. I still don't see it often these days." JT can tell he has Ania's ear. "But I tell you and I would put this on my soul, he loves you and just wait, y'all going to be alright."

Ania looks at him then smiles. "Thank you JT." Then they hug, and he walks out the door to his car into the darkness under the illumination from the driveway lights. JT starts up the Range, and when he starts to move away from the house, there is a car approaching slowly, and he looks through his smoke black-tinted windows over into the passing car, and he sees a man driving the car that he recognizes. JT slows down and pulls into a vacant parking spot along the street and can't believe his eyes. Bill has just got out of the car and is walking towards the house.

"Ain't this a bitch?" JT says. He picks up his phone and dials Larenz. "Damn it L pick up."

Dancing

JT has no idea but Larenz is taking some alone time to think about everything happening, and he's already decided it's about time he faces things head on. So, he takes his car and drives over to see Lisa at Marbles; his phone starts to ring, but he decides to let it go. Immediately after Larenz parks his car he is surprised to see Lisa. She is walking in the parking lot to her car, and she gets inside, rolls down the windows then gets back out the car and stands sill until she hears music start to play.

Larenz squints his eyes to get a better look and can see Lisa begin to dance all alone; identically to the way she did with him so long ago, when they were in Chicago in the same month of September; right there under the illumined parking lot. Larenz turns off his car, rolls down the windows and can hear that she still likes to dance to the Afrobeat sound that is always pumped heavy in Lagos, Nigeria. Instantly it brings back many memories for Larenz because they would always request the same rhythm of music when they were together and dance the entire night away. Larenz keeps his eyes on Lisa dancing and remembers her movements and it's like nothing has changed. Her sway is still smooth and effortless while still being light on her toes. Her dress is flowing with the wind in unison with the music like a dream. At first Larenz doesn't move from the car as he watches her dance; then, without even realizing it, he is standing in the parking lot directly behind Lisa, visualizing dancing with her. He is seconds from moving in from behind to join her when the music stops and she is no longer dancing.

Lisa is surprised. "Larenz? What are you..."

His smile is warm with remembrance from the past and he attempts to shake off his mindset. "Lisa, uhh hey, I see you still have it. Out here tearing it up in the parking lot," he says.

She takes a long deep breath then says, "Well, if you haven't forgotten, when the mood comes, I'm going to dance, Larenz, plus it's my birthday. I wanted to celebrate a bit; you know."

He looks directly in her eyes and says, "Yeah, I remember. You still have it, that's for sure and hey, happy birthday."

"Is that right?"

"Absolutely."

She pauses then straightens out her dress and hair all in one swoop. "So, what is it Larenz? Ania send you over here on an upset wifey move to come cuss me out?"

Larenz is taken back a bit and puts both hands in the air like he's under arrest, but smiles just the same. "No, no, nothing like that. I just wanted to talk, that's all."

Lisa takes a long pause and looks at Larenz and he doesn't understand the look in her eyes. "You're lying." Lisa storms off back into the club leaving Larenz standing in the parking lot all alone. Larenz only calls out to her one time, then he walks back to his car and sits inside for about fifteen minutes, completely isolated, thinking about his next move, not even letting the constant ringing of his phone take him out of his thoughts.

–

Lisa is now in her office, back at her desk, playing urban soul on her Pandora station. She vaguely hears a knock on her door, then it opens, and a bit of the rap music playing out on the dance floor of the club leaks in for a few seconds before the door is shut, and Larenz cautiously walks in and he notices Lisa's eyes directly on him.

"Oh hey, Zoe told me to come on back." Larenz is looking around her office tentatively. He is definitely on egg shells.

Lisa doesn't respond right away. "So, you're not here 'cause Ania sent you?"

"Nope."

"Let me guess. You're here to critique me on my poetry skills? Did they not fit into your establishments guidelines and your bestselling status Larenz?"

Larenz plays her game and even waits a beat before he responds. "Nah…." he sings. "Not at all. Actually, it was quite provoking. Very powerful and insightful. Gwendolyn Brooks - esque you know?"

"Yeah right, get the heck outta here. Don't dis my girl like that. But I tell you it was over twenty-years in the making, if you don't mind me saying."

Larenz moves his eyes away from a painting on her wall and looks at Lisa. "I don't mind at all. No worries, do you."

She says, "You know if you don't mind me saying; I was wondering if you would come by or continue to hide."

"Me, hide? Never that. You have to know someone is out here looking for you, in order to do that." There is an awkward silence. Larenz even has a chance to walk to the other side of her office and look at the Novica African Masks hanging on the wall; before he says, "What's going on Lisa? Care to explain coming over to my club and laying that heavy poem down in front of everyone, most importantly my family and friends?"

She sighs. "Basically, you mean, Ania don't you?"

"Yeah, for the most part, yeah." Larenz can feel his phone buzz again, but he doesn't check it.

"Well….if you really must know. I wanted her to know that, what we had, was much, much more than what you have led everyone to believe what it really was."

Larenz is shaking his head in amazement. "In your mind, what we had, right? I have my point of view and feelings surrounding the matter too, don't I. And how do you know, what I told her, anyway?"

Lisa delivers a tight-laced smile without appearing haughty. "Some of us, from the block still talk, Larenz. Some of us, still keep in touch, you know? Some of us, pick up the phone and say hi, happy birthday and so forth."

"Aight', okay I hear you."

Lisa is blunt and nippy. "Bill, he told me, if you must know."

Larenz thinks on her words. "What? That played-out fool, knows nothing about what comes out of my mouth."

"Doesn't seem that way to me. He apparently knows someone who knows what comes out of Ania's mouth or she's telling him herself."

"Look, you know, we were young back in the day. And I don't need to remind you, how that whole thing works when you're out here looking for what you want to do with your life. And with who? I mean, looking back on it, it's a wonder any of us has made it this far in life."

"But you're a wordsmith, Mr. Bestseller, always have been and you know how to put words, phrases and things, all together, and bunch them up for a woman, where she could put in her mind that what you say or said to her is the complete gospel. That's what you can do. No, let me rephrase that Mr. Author Poetry man, that's what you have always done and it's definitely what you did to me. My GOD you have your own club that started off as a pure poetry establishment with you selling cold drinks out of a cooler, that has thrived in this city for years."

He is thinking about her words. "Look, it doesn't matter."

"Matters to me."

"Okay, put it this way– what I'm trying to say is, why does all this matter, now Lisa, after all this time?"

"It matters to me, because I want to know that I was wanted. Believe it or not, there's not been one man in my life after you, all this time." Larenz has a look of disbelief on his face. "Honestly."

"But you....?" He turns his body slightly and points out towards the club.

"Yeah, I know, I have Zoe. And thank GOD for her. You want to know how she came along?"

"Look, I know the process."

"But my process, was meeting him once, sleeping with him once, not knowing his name after a drunken night at the club-that type of process."

"Hey, I didn't know..."

"Because you never asked, Larenz."

"This is...I never knew to ask?"

"Listen to what I am telling you. I've never been in a relationship, beside what you say, we didn't have. All I have to draw from is what we had, way back when. Do you know at my age, I have never received a gift from a man? Not even a thank you for a good fuck note. Not one."

Larenz pauses and thinks about her words. "Hey, look, I'm sorry."

"It's nothing you did directly. But just know that you played a part in my feelings. The way I think about men, the way I guess they think women are disposable. You are a part of that after all these years and it's important to me that you know."

Larenz starts and stops to comment a few times then says, "Again, I'm sorry for your feelings. But I'm married now. I love my wife, and I'm always going to do anything to protect her, that's on GOD."

"I understand and respect you for that."

"Just know, if I can do anything to change your opinion about me, I'll do it. I know how powerful words are, and believe me, I didn't do those things intentionally because I don't like negative vibes about me running out here, especially when I know when what I've done has hurt someone else. Tell me, what can I do?"

Lisa doesn't respond right away then smiles. "Have a drink with me Larenz." She pulls out another glass and the sound of Lisa pouring his drink is passionate. "Yes, have a drink with me."

–

So, that night Larenz ends up having more than one drink with Lisa. She pours two and they have a healthy, in-depth conversation. Lisa is nonstop catching him up on the last twenty-plus years of her life. This discussion is way more in-depth than the coffee shop meet-up. They have a lot in common, especially with both only having one child. Her experiences are much different from Larenz's because she is single, and more than once, she reminds him of that, and all he can do is agree and give thanks that he nor Ania didn't have to raise Jacob alone because single parenting is a hell of a job. One thing is for sure, he doesn't realize that she is so tight with Bill. On the outside looking in, Larenz has a feeling that he kept in touch with Lisa just to see if she has ever run into him because more than a few times, she lets him know that when Bill calls, he has never resisted asking about him and Ania. But Lisa never has news for him because she really didn't know and has been so busy with her own life. All in all, it was a very good conversation, and they both agreed not to harbor any ill-will between them. Larenz apologizes again for, in her eyes, leading her on back in the day, and she tells him she is sorry for blowing up the spot in his club. At the end of their conversation, they agree there is no reason to be strangers, now that their offspring are preparing to tie the knot, and they promise to make things smooth for their new family union and beyond.

Question

The next morning, back in the guesthouse, Nicole is smiling in the mirror for an extended amount of time, and she begins to speak. "Are you sure? This is such a surprise. Are you sure this is what you want? You mean the world to me as well, as a matter of fact, I can't live without you either. Of course, I'll marry you sweetheart, of course, I will." Afterwards, she takes a few seconds to look at herself in the mirror again. She raises her hand and caresses her face, then smiles. There is a knock at the door, and she answers.

It's Ania. "Hey there lady, good morning." Nicole smiles, greets her, and lets her in. Ania looks around. "Were you on the phone? I thought I heard someone talking?"

Indirectly Nicole looks at her and hopes Ania can't tell she's being allusive. "No, just me singing. Humming mostly. How are you today? Did you get a good night's rest?"

Ania sits down at the small kitchen table she hand-picked at Hobby Lobby. When she first laid eyes on the table she knew it would be a perfect fit for the guesthouse. She runs her hand over the top of it just to remember its smooth touch, then halfway smiles. "I slept okay, not as well as I would've liked, but hey, it was rest and I get another chance today to make it better than yesterday."

"Now, that's a perfect way to look at it."

"Yeah, I'm trying. There are plenty worse things that can be happening besides a fling of your husbands past showing up and showing her ass, for all to see."

Nicole chuckles. "Yeah, you're right, friend." Nicole turns on the water faucet to make coffee and asks Ania if she wants any. Ania declines; she is meeting Jacob for brunch a little later. Ania tells Nicole she found out last night that Jacob is engaged. She didn't get all the details because of everything that was going on.

Nicole says, "You know, you and Larenz have been together forever. I know I haven't been around you two on the daily for years, and I am sure over all the years you two have been together that you have gotten into spats. I mean after all these years you have to, right?"

"Girl, yes. You already know, it's always something but we always give and take, you know, compromise. To be blunt, it hasn't been an argument, but we have been going back and forth on trying to get away from it all for a vacation. Just us two, enjoying one another, but he has been swamped with work but he keeps making promises; and it's very irritating."

Nicole scoops coffee into the maker and looks at Ania. She knows what she is going to say will be touching on a delicate subject, and she makes sure her tone and delivery are on point. "If you don't mind me saying, sis, it just seems to me that you and Larenz have been together so long that if Halle Berry walked in for him and Denzel for you, it shouldn't be able to break y'all up. I mean what you two have, people only dream of. And for someone to be able to just walk in and disrupt what you have really throws me for a loop."

Ania says, "I receive that. I really do. But the thing is, it's just not someone. It's a person I know Larenz had feelings for at one time. He had a relationship with her when we separated for that short period and probably for some time after. I know it's petty to some, but for me, it's not."

Nicole says, "In the scheme of things to me, it's very petty because of all the time you two have spent together. I mean you were even together before you were married. You've spent your whole life practically together."

"Yeah, you're right," Ania says.

"But it's even more serious than that."

"What do you mean?"

"I'm just saying, I remember, and I'm going way back now, to how hurt Larenz was when you hooked up with Bill. He was really hurt behind that, and to add it all up, he took you back after you and Bill did the deed."

Ania pushes away from the table a bit. "The deed, what deed?"

"C'mon, now sis– it's me you're talking to."

"No, I'm serious Nicole–I don't know what you're talking about?"

Nicole shakes her head. "Listen, one of the things Larenz would always say, when the gang used to sit around and conversate, is that, he wouldn't take you back if he found out you were intimate with Bill. And when he found out you were, it must have been very hard for him to get over it and take you back–that's all I'm saying."

"I can't believe what you're saying to me Nicole?"

"I don't mean any malice; of course, I'm just stating some facts. Larenz did something very few men would do."

–

Minutes later, Ania enters the kitchen through the back door of the house, and Larenz walks in from the hallway at the same exact time. They stop and lock eyes.

Larenz looks her up and down and can tell she is steaming. He asks, "You okay?"

Ania says, "Yes, what would make you ask that?"

"Just looks like you're upset about something."

Ania swipes her hand through her hair and puts her hands on her hips. "No, I'm good."

Larenz says, "Good, and good morning."

"Same to you."

Larenz has to walk past Ania to get to the coffee pot and she moves out the way. "Coffee?"

"No, thank you," she says back. Ania just watches Larenz, the way he is moving. So careful and punctilious, and she knows something is awry. "You were with her last night, weren't you?"

He stops cold right before his cup of coffee touches his lips and then he sighs. "I saw her, yes."

"And?"

"And I told her how I really feel about her."

"Excuse me, you did what?"

He takes a sip of his coffee first. "Yeah, I went over to her club, and I told her I have absolutely no feelings for her and that what she did, coming into the club like that, was wrong."

Ania still has her hands on her hips watching him wait for her response, barely being able to drink his coffee. "Negro, please. You come in here the next morning after some bitch, you were involved with over twenty-years ago, professes her love for you on the stage of our club, who you swear you didn't know lived here, and tell me that mess? Did you fuck her? You can tell me, we're all grown here."

"Ania? What the hell is wrong with you? No, didn't you even listen to anything I said?"

"I heard you, but you're not saying anything. So, if what you told her is true, why didn't you come home last night?"

"I went back to the club. Fell asleep on that couch after a few drinks."

"Don't give me that, you mean after a few drinks with her, right?"

Larenz is quiet for a beat; he doesn't want to go through this and quickly remembers it wasn't even this hard last night communicating with Lisa. "Right, we had a few."

"I knew it."

"Okay, but that's it. She wanted to explain to me why she did the poem; she says my actions in the past are a part of the hurt she has inside. And you know, I can truly see, where she's coming from."

"Oh, really?"

"Yes, I can see."

"Well, I hope you can see, where I'm coming from? Do you understand that, as your wife, I might be a little confused as to what the hell is going on?"

"Oh, yeah, I can see that too."

"And you should, because know it or not, I don't have to take this."

"What is wrong with you? Take what? I'm just reacting to what's happening and trying to piece it all together."

"All I'm saying is, I don't have to take this and remember what I am telling you, okay?"

Larenz puts down his coffee cup. "Seriously, what the hell is wrong with you Ania? You walk into the kitchen, and obviously, something is wrong, and you won't admit it. Then you're upset because I tell you the truth about where I was last night, and now you're talking about you don't have to take this. What is really going on?" Larenz notices Ania's eyes are becoming moist. She is in pain and he walks over to her.

"No, no Larenz I'm good." He steps back after he tries to hug her, because she places her hands up into his chest so that he can't. "Look, I want to know something, and all I want is the truth. So much happening right now that I can't tell what is true or not, but tell me something."

"Sure, what is it?"

"I want to know Larenz, I want to know if you would have married me, if I would have slept with Bill?" Larenz doesn't understand, and she can see it in his eyes. "Tell me the truth, would you have married me Larenz?"

"What are you saying Ania? Are you standing here telling me that now? Is it because Lisa rolls up in our lives and you want to come clean or something? "You tell me, why you're asking?"

"I'm asking because I want to know."

"And I want to know why the hell you want to know after all these years? You know what? This is asinine Ania. I have to go. I have a busy day." Larenz starts to walk out and he doesn't stop when she calls out after him.

Sweat it Out

Ideally, it's supposed to be a day of relaxation, and lots of deep breaths, just putting everything in perspective and reducing everything in mind, to decrease anything attempting to be of overwhelming importance in Larenz and JT's lives. That is why Larenz is headed to the gym to meet up with JT, to switch it up, and talk business with a chilled, light workout session. Larenz really needs to exercise and relax his muscles after his morning with Ania and night with

Lisa. He is so taken aback by the events that he can't even wait to get in the gym to vibe with JT, so, he calls his boy Isaiah, to get some added clarity.

Isaiah answers like on the third ring. "Nigga, didn't I tell you to never call me when I'm getting my hair cut?"

Larenz looks into his phone then places it back on his ear. "What? I'm on my way to the gym, but I need to talk first," Larenz makes clear.

Isaiah is sitting in the shop. He gets up from his seat and mentions to the barber that he'll be right outside on the phone and to not let any of the wannabe rappers take his spot because he'll be watching through the window to make sure. When he gets completely out of the shop he answers Larenz. "That's right, it was highlighted on the text I sent your black ass when I sent you my new do not disturb schedule. Didn't you get it after you disturbed me the last time?"

Larenz covers his mouth. "Oh, I was supposed to read that shit?"

"Hell, yes you were supposed to read the shit. It's my life; I have reclaimed my time as a husband, father, and hectic business owner. I am now relaxing and maintaining mine. And since you didn't read it, nukka you better not call me tomorrow because I'll be at my book club meeting with over seventy-five women in attendance, and guess what, guess what?"

"What, what is it Isaiah?"

"I'm the one and only male in this joint. They need my gotdamn opinion on everything, so I don't need to be interrupted by your ass. I will be spitting knowledge on Langston Hughes' joint *Laughing to Keep from Crying,* you got it?"

Larenz says, "Dig, now I know why they let you in their club."

"Fool, what're you talking about?"

"I'm just saying they needed someone "Simple" to break down the stories for them."

"Aye, man bump you, you hear me? Just because you're an author don't mean I can't dissect some things for the ladies." Isaiah looks around his surroundings then back in the shop to make sure his spot is still secure. "So, what's up? You calling me to tell me you done slipped up and poked Lisa…Lisa?"

"What, now why would you say that? Don't you know Ania been pressing me about it too, after I spent most of last night with her?"

"Wait, wait one gotdamn minute black man. You spent most of last night with Lisa? I outta' beat your…"

"Nah, slow down. Look, last night was a trip."

Isaiah says, "I'm listening and definitely want to hear about it. Hey, does she still got that little, big-booty; or nah?"

"Bruh, this ain't bout her little, big-booty; but hell yes." Larenz can hear Isaiah laughing through the line.

Isaiah pushes, "I knew it, I just knew it. All she used to eat was red beans and rice with salad. Pow!"

"Dig, at the club last night she strolls in and the whole crew is there– Ania, Nicole, JT, Jill, Kerry, Bill and Jacob and his girl, which is a whole different story."

"Who Jacob—different story? Don't tell me he done hooked up with a man-girl?"

Larenz says, "I should just jump through this line and onto one of these 5G towers to find out exactly where you're at, and just swoop down and slap the daylight out of you. Hell nah. Nothing like that."

"Well....you are in the ....."

"Don't say it, cause it ain't like that in The A bruh. I keep telling everybody, we got real ones down here making it happen and my son just so happens to be one of those real ones who loves the ladies."

"So, get to it. You're perplexed cause Ania rightfully so, wants to know if you dug into Lisa, right?"

"Right."

"Well, did you?"

"No, man, I'm not saying it again. Listen, we were all in the club, Lisa walks in and gets on stage to do a poem."

"Did they dim the lights and all?"

Larenz can tell he's smiling in remembrance. "Yeah, you know how we do."

"Go 'head, I'm listening, but I'm about to light up."

"Thought you quit?"

"I always smoke me a cigar after my cut, but I'm going to start this one now." He starts to light up and turns to look in the barber shop again to make sure his spot is still intact.

Larenz continues, "So, she gets up on the stage and reads this poem about how she still thinks about me, and what could have been, and she can't shake it, and so on."

"And you spent most of the night with her and didn't nudge up in her? I don't know. That's a hard one to believe."

"Nope. She turned the whole night upside down with her poem. Ania went off and everybody at the table was looking at me silly. I can't even get Ania to believe that I just found out she was in Atlanta."

"See, what did I tell you? I told you to tell her as soon as you found out."

"That's not all, during all this, Jacob tells me that he is getting married to Lisa's daughter, Zoe."

"Wait….what?"

"Yes, it looks like we're going to be kinfolk with Lisa. Can you believe it?"

Isaiah blows out a plume of smoke. "Unbelievable."

Larenz says, "I know, right? But check this out, so during our conversation: she breaks it all down and tells me that she never could get over the words I would say to her, but now knows she has to because I'm married, but I hurt her to the core. And I understand how she feels man, I really do."

"Always told you to stop with all that slick lyrical ish and writing them damn poems to the ladies."

"Yeah, so what should I do now?"

Isaiah blows out another cloud of smoke from his cigar. "Bruh, I don't know, you done stepped in it. All I can tell your black ass is to keep it "Simple." He looks in the shop and his barber is waving him in. "Hey, gotta' go I'll hit you back and you better read my new schedule; I sent it to you for a reason." Larenz doesn't even get the chance to discuss the question Ania asked him earlier in the day, which was the most important topic of all at the moment.

–

Now at the gym it's hard for Larenz to relax and enjoy the sauna. JT picks up on it.

"Bruh, you need to relax." JT reaches for the ladle sitting in the wooden bucket full of water in the sauna, fills it full then pours it over the rocks and watches as the steam is made from the heat on the rocks. "There we go, there we go, more steam to clear these toxins out my boy." He looks at Larenz and says, "You good?" Larenz tells him yes. "Well, you're not acting like it. But since we're supposed to be in here talking business while relaxing. Everything is looking good. We already identified everything that needs to be prepared on the commercial, and I paid those contract inspectors their fee. I'm just waiting to hear from you about last night's take, so we can start to decide what percentage of that can be added to what we already have to cover the commercial."

Larenz says, "Oh yeah, it's all good. There aren't going to be any problems; the house was packed and should be until they get the hell out the club."

JT says, "Cool, another smart business deal we made with Bill."

"Yeah, money wise, it was smart. But it seems like nothing but drama since he rolled-up in town."

"You're right things have turned up a notch or two."

"Just sayin' ever since he arrived, things just been out of whack. I told you this guy had a bad omen on his ass."

"Yeah, but all this could just be life. I mean, you just now finding out Lisa's in town, now your son is about to marry her daughter, and your wife's trippin' cause Lisa's back; you didn't know she was here, and that damn poem. Damn that was foul."

"That's not it."

"It should be, what else you need to be going on? That would be enough for me."

"This morning, Ania asked me if I would have still married her if I knew she slept with Bill before we were married."

"Hold up; she asked you that?" Larenz doesn't answer; right back and JT has time to think by putting more water on the rocks with the ladle. "On soul, that would make me feel a certain kind of way."

"That's where I am. I'm so messed up behind it I can barely sweat, and it's over a hundred degrees up in this sauna."

Looky Here

Larenz and JT only spend about fifteen more minutes in the sauna chopping it up. Afterwards they go directly to the car in the parking lot. As soon as they are comfortable, JT nods over to Larenz; to look and see who just walked right past them on the other side of the street. "Well, looky here looky here," JT says.

Larenz says, "Welp, I think it's time to get on this youngins' ass, don't you think?"

"I do. I really do," JT tells him.

They step out of the car, and Larenz calls out to Calvin's son, Cam. He takes a few steps before he stops after Larenz calls him for the second time. "You got a minute?"

Cam looks around. "What's up Unc? I'm running late. How bout we chat later?"

"Not good for me," Larenz says, "How about we chat right now?"

Cam looks around again. "That means right now, Cam," JT tells him. Cam mumbles something under his breath and starts to walk over. He is wearing a nice pair of jeans, sneakers and has a fresh haircut.

"Looking good," Larenz says, then he looks at JT, "Don't he look good JT?"

"Shining and profiling," JT mentions. "Did you just hit that lotto my boy?" Cam looks down at his fit and smiles a bit and tells them no.

"But how you doin'? That's what I want to know," Larenz says.

"I'm good, just trying to get to the next level."

Larenz gets straight to it. "What level you talking? Like a tier level in prison or some shit?"

He says, "What? Nah, not me Unc."

"Oh yeah, that's where you're going because I heard you got something of mine that I gave to Calvin." Cam kind of pokes out his bottom lip and shakes his head no. "Well, you know us, we're not sugar-coating anything, and I already see you're setting up to lie, so where's the money, Cam?"

"What money? I don't know what you're talkin' bout?"

Larenz looks at JT, and says, "I knew his lying ass was about to lie."

JT says, "I could have told you that, he doesn't even look us in the eye. Can't no man keep eye connection with another man once he steals from his very own father. It's fucked up and making me mad. Where's the money?"

Cam squints his eyes and puffs out his chest. "Look, you two out here thinking you're still talking to an eight-year-old boy or something. But you're not, I'm grown so change your tone?"

Larenz looks at JT and they smile. Larenz says, "Oh, listen to Mr. Man here."

JT says, "I hear him barking."

Larenz looks him up and down then points out. "Mr. Man, who is still living with his parents. Mr. Man, who is stealing money off of tables that he knows good damn well he shouldn't put his hands on. Mr. Man, who is not giving two OG's, who practically brought his ass up with any proper respect, and who, I might add, won't think twice about thrashing that ass, right here on the street."

JT says, "Oh yeah, this is the type of workout we need right here my boy, since the one inside didn't get the job done."

Larenz says, "Seems like that little bit of money, you got—done split your head up Cam. Remember we know you, know every soft bone in your soft ass body."

JT says, "So, you're the one who better watch his tone because you're talking to grown men."

"Look here," Larenz says, "Calvin told me you got him for some money. I gave him that money because he earned it and that don't sit right with us, so I'm going to need to get it back. Honestly, tell me how do you think you can just take it anyway? Something has your head twisted for real."

Cam says, "First of all, I ain't say, I took it."

"But you did," JT pushes.

"And if I did?"

Larenz says, "If you did, be clear we're getting it back."

JT says, "And you say you didn't again we still getting it back. So, where is it?"

"Man…I only stopped to talk to y'all outta' respect, but I don't have to tell you shit."

Larenz tells him, "So, I see you're out here trying to get your grown man on. I guess that's how we're about to treat you because evidently being empathic and having concern for your slimy, acting ass is not what you want. So, check this here out, from this point on we treating you like a regular nobody on the block. Is that cool?"

JT says, "Damn sure cool with me."

Cam's eyes widened. "Look, ain't nobody out here helping me. I'm out here on my own trying to make it."

Larenz says, "Don't you have a job?"

"A job? Hell nah," he says.

"What you mean hell nah? How are you going to take care of yourself?" JT wants to know.

"I ain't working for nobody," he says.

"And if that's the way you feel, I feel sorry for your life because everybody works for somebody, you just don't know it yet," Larenz tells him. "Cam, Calvin can't keep carrying you. So, this is what we're going to do. You know the commercial building downtown we purchased?"

"Yeah, who doesn't."

"Go down there, walk in, and tell the site manager Gregg, I sent you and to put you to work."

"And give Calvin, his money back," JT says.

"Look, I told you I don't have no money."

JT is losing patience. "Youngin', I know we taught you a lot growing up, but if you say that one more time, I'm going to walk over to you and knock you clean the fuck out."

Cam is looking at Larenz hoping he will intervene and he does. "Let me tell you a little story Cam, there aren't a lot of things JT and I have carried over from our fathers, GOD rest their souls. We eat better, we work out, take care of our families and don't have an excuse for a got damn thing. But, what we still do keep alive and well, just like them, is the will and honor to take a man's son that we know, who is out here in the streets acting like he has no sense, and beat his ass every time he needs it and think nothing of it while doing it. So, if I were you, I'd have myself down there at eight in the morning, or we will be looking for you, and trust me, when we catch up to you, it's on sight."

"Right, my pops not going to let y'all touch me."

JT tells him, "Your father is our brother, don't do what we're telling you and I bet you, he'll have no problem with what we do."

Brunch

Ania and Jacob haven't had the chance to sit and talk about everything going on. They both love downtown and the essence of the city; so, they meet at Café Intermezzo. Jacob has scored a table close to the sidewalk, and he is genuinely happy to see his mom on her way to their table. He places his phone down and greets her with a hug. They order and have a very nice conversation during their brunch, then dessert comes out, cheesecake, with cherries on top. It's not long after, they get into what has been on their minds.

"Ma, just to let you know, I don't think dad knew Zoe's mom was in town after all these years," Jacob says.

Ania takes her eyes off her cheesecake. "You really think so?"

"I really don't. I mean, Zoe and I were really messed up behind the whole thing. I can tell you that dad was trying to tell me something when I came into the club with her, but then all of a sudden, when he was talking, Lisa appeared on stage."

Ania puts down her fork. "Oh, please don't say her name in the middle of my dessert."

He laughs a bit. "Can't run from it ma, it happened."

"Now, when have you ever seen your mama run from anything?"

"I haven't."

"Okay then, it's just that no one knows what your father and I went through trying to get past her to get where we are."

Jacob is cautious. "That goes for that Bill guy too, right?"

"Bill?"

"Yeah, I met him at the club. Kind of a loud-mouth."

"You're right about that."

"I'm just saying, so dad had to go through some things too, right?"

"Yeah, you're right." Ania takes another swipe into her cheesecake, but for the first time, not with the same care as her previous delicate digs into her treat; you can even hear the fork hit the plate as it slices through. Then she remembers her conversation with Nicole before she places her cake in her mouth. "So, what have *you* heard about Bill?"

Jacob seems to be finished with his dessert and pushes it away. "Ma it's kind of difficult to get into. I'm saying, it was a long time ago—right?"

"A very long time ago, before you were born."

"See, that makes it weird to me. Knowing that you and dad, at a time were together, then not together. Then he and Zoe's mom getting together, and you and Bill doing your thing, then you and dad getting back together. It's all a little too much. I know it's your history and all, but all this is new to me. All I know of you is what I know of you, and that's how I want to keep it."

She smiles. "Wow, I didn't know you knew that much about us?"

"Yeah, I guess Zoe has heard it, and then that poem Lisa did on stage. It really got me and Zoe talking about it because it's got us, in an awkward situation too."

"So, you two, have discussed all this?"

"We had too," he chuckles. "It was bananas, that night, for a short time, we thought we were freakn' siblings or something."

She laughs. "What?"

"Yes, just look at the circumstances, we were going through; it's a birthday I will never forget."

"So, y'all went to Lisa hunh, to find out?"

"Yeah, had to. It was intense."

Ania puts her fork down. "Well, is there anything else you need to know because I know a little bit about went on between all of us, too."

Jacob doesn't respond right back. It's like his silence throws the whole conversation into a loop and forces Ania to prod him. "Well, it's just that Zoe and I were talking, and she said that if dad knew you and Bill," he looks at her then nudges his head and she doesn't respond, so he does the same repeatedly and at the same time, widens his eyes. "That he would have never asked you to move to Atlanta with him and start this life y'all built together."

Ania only smiles because it's the second time today she has heard the same pathetic gibberish. "Oh, she told you that?"

"Yes, she mentioned it."

"I guess she got that from her mom then because there's no way she would know because she wasn't even freakn' walking the earth right?"

"Yeah, I guess…"

"Well, that's not true Jacob. It never happened."

Jacob thinks for a minute. "So, you think he would have married you if it was true?" Ania looks directly at Jacob and doesn't answer right off. She just wanders off into another sphere. "Ma, you okay?"

She snaps out of it. "Yeah, yes boy, I'm fine. Quite some mess huh, such a mess after all these years."

"Yeah, I know this guy shows up and everybody got something to say about the past."

"Crazy," she says, then pushes her plate away a bit and mentions she needs to be leaving soon, and Jacob turns and looks for their waitress; she says, "You know that −DNA is real right?"

Jacob says, "What do you mean by that?"

"Well, like my mama and them use to say, the apple doesn't fall far from the tree."

Jacob finally gets his waitress' attention, motions for the check, then looks back at Ania. "Apple?"

"It means that your offspring are very similar to their parents, and now that you're engaged……" She sees him smile. "It's just that you better be certain you know that what she brings to your relationship a lot of it, she has learned from her mom."

Jacob nods his head in agreement. "Yeah, now that's true."

"And Zoe not coming from a two-parent household might be quite a difference for her."

"What do you mean?"

"I'm talking about relating and being with a man, her husband−son, you. Working together. It's much more different than what she has seen growing up. You might have a different perspective on how things are done as a family unit because you have seen me and your dad move. As far as I know she has never had a male in her life, I suppose since your dad didn't mention to me that Lisa was married or anything."

"Yeah, yeah you're right."

"See, that's what I'm saying you witnessed two people working things out together. She hasn't; it has always been her mother doing everything and making all the decisions without any input. But you've seen it a whole different way. And the way she handles things and goes about situations more than likely will not be the same way you have learned to do it."

"Wow, that's deep. I haven't even thought about it like that."

"And I am just talking about you two together, you know? I'm not talking about bringing a child into the situation, it gets even deeper then. You do want children, right? You do plan on giving me one grandchild at least, don't you?" She smiles.

He smiles back at her. "Sure do; that's the plan," Jacob lets her know, then it's time to pay the check.

Broke My Heart

Hours later, Jacob is at home, sitting on his couch with the television on, but not particularly watching it; he has smoked half of a blunt to relax his mind and contemplate on his life's path. He's proud of himself. He's an engaged young black man with a college degree, a good job as an engineer, without a criminal record, and a possibility of taking over Nickels if he ever wants to, according to Larenz, so his father can get back to banging out a few books. A few times while Jacob sits on the couch, he looks up. He can't believe that a car maintenance commercial has been running back-to-back for more than an hour, but Jacob is so buzzed and deep in his thoughts he doesn't grab the remote and turn it off. When a text comes through on his phone, it somewhat brings him out his relaxing moment; he reads it and then gets up to answer the door.

His grin is wide and he says, "What's up baby?" He lets Zoe in. Right away Jacob notices her leftovers in a bag from Slutty Vegan. She tells him hello kisses him on the cheek. "How come you didn't use your key?"

"Aww, damn, I do have your key, don't I fiancé?" Her smile widens then she extends her arm and looks at her ring.

"If you don't get yourself in here," he says and they walk over to the couch in front of the television with the freakn' commercial still playing.

Zoe looks around at the atmosphere. She spots some weed on the table yet to be rolled. "I see you're just chilling? Hey, you hear about the Rico charges piling up? That's crazy, right?"

"Yeah, nobody is the winner in this one, you know?"

"Facts. So, you got your smoke all out and things. I see you."

"Yeah, no big deal just a few hits to mellow out."

"I see," she says; then gets comfortable on the couch. Zoe grabs the remote and flips to the channel guide on television for something different to watch. She decides on a movie where two young females are talking about being like their parents in relationships. And because it's on, Jacob half-way tunes in after Zoe puts her hand in his lap.

"Hmm, interesting," she continues watching, and Jacob looks at her, he tunes in a bit more to see what it's all about.

He gets the jest of the conversation on the tube and says, "You know, my mother was saying something like that to me today."

She lifts her butt off the couch turns towards him all in one motion, still holding the remote. "She did?" Jacob is still watching the television and just nods yes so she just starts watching the show again. After a few seconds, she repeats the same movement on the couch, this time she puts the remote down next to the weed. "So, she was talking about me and my mom then huh?"

"I don't know Zoe, it was like one of those mother and son talks where she tries to fill my brain with a bunch of life's experiences, so I don't make the same mistakes so she can say see, I told you."

"I see, we get engaged and she starts to talk about mistakes?"

"What?"

She doesn't look at Jacob but says, "You heard me because my mother did it, too."

Almost an entire scene in the movie ends, and Jacob says, "Wow, so your mother thinks I can repeat the actions of my pops? The apple falls from the tree?"

She turns to him, "Your mother said that about me?"

"Zoe, my mother probably said the same thing your mother said about me. So, let's not do the, what she said, game. We know our parents have talked to us, about us; that is pretty natural if you ask me."

"Oh, really?"

"No doubt. I'm going to talk to our son, if he ever gets married. Come to think about it, I haven't even talked to pops yet; I know his ass has something to say, with all that wisdom he kicks."

"So, you're going to talk to our son?"

Jacob smiles at the idea of it all. "Hell, yeah, that's what pops do."

Zoe is stern. "What if I wanted to do it?"

Jacob says, "Do what?"

"Talk to him…"

"About getting married and starting a family?"

"Yes, me."

"I mean you could. My mom just talked–to me. But it's damn sure not the way I know pops will. I mean it was kind of awkward with mom, because she's a woman too and there is a fine line in conversations when you talk to your moms. But pops is a different story, we get in it. Dissecting, analyzing, all the layered facts concerning a situation. I mean really chopping it up." Jacob smiles.

"Really now?"

"Exactly, I'm actually anxious to hear what my O' Gee has to say."

"So, is that how it will be when we get married? You decide what we're going to do then, we'll do it?"

"Are you serious, right now?"

"Yes."

"No, I mean we will talk about things, you know discuss situations."

"Then do what you say? Got it."

"Okay, what're you getting at Zoe?"

"Just saying my mom said that's the way your dad used to be. He was always low key about his, not wanting my mother to tell others they were together and didn't like when his name was in her mouth."

"Oh, is that right?"

"Said, he was in complete control of every situation between them."

"Maybe he was just in control of his life? Have you thought about that? See, to be honest with you, this is one of the things I was thinking about when I blazed up."

"What?"

"This, this conversation, I was thinking about if you have a lot of your mother's tendencies and thoughts and how that materializes on how you will be with me."

"Damn, is that all?"

"No, I mean it would really be nice to know now how you really feel about a man leading a family since you didn't grow up with one."

"Oh, is that some kind of strike on me 'cause my mother raised me on her own?"

"No, it's not a strike Zoe, it's just facts."

"Well, you're acting like it's a bad thing or something?" Zoe gets up from the couch.

"Where you goin'?"

"You're making me mad."

Jacob reaches his hand out to her, trying to grab her hand. "C'mon sit back down. We're just talking, don't you think we need to talk about all this before we really have to talk about it when we're married?" Zoe thinks about sitting down, then finally does, and Jacob says, "Look, you already told me what your mother said about me. So, can you be really truthful and tell me that you haven't been thinking about it? When did she talk to you anyway?"

Zoe is mad and pouty at the same time. "The other night," she sings. "But I already told you most of what she said, except the part about how I should watch out and make sure that you don't have all the control of the money and finances because your father is tight."

Jacob laughs and rubs his hands on top of his head. "Wow, how would she know that? When they were seeing each other —they were young. They were just starting out in life and were broke as hell."

"You asked me what she said. Now what did your mom say about me?"

"Nothing really, I already told you. Just that the apple doesn't fall far from the tree and I should stay woke about that and maybe you don't know about family dynamics."

"Oh, oh, so your mother thinks I don't?"

"I mean...she has a point. You've never had a father in the house. To be truthful, where's the lie?"

"So, the bottom line is, your mother doesn't want me to be like my mom and my mom don't want you to be like your dad."

"I guess, I mean, I don't know, shit."

She starts to take the ring off. "You know what, here, take the ring, not doing this."

"Zeee, are you really feeling like that right now? I mean we're just talking."

"I don't care, the vibes not right, and I ain't going to marry you like this."

"My vibe not right? So, you're just gonna' raise up and break my heart?"

"I guess so 'cause you broke my heart, too. The vibes and this conversation–geez who wants to live like this together forever."

He sits and thinks, "Okay fine, let's just forget about it."

Jacob watches Zoe remove her ring then place it on the table. "Yeah, okay fine. I think it's for the best Jacob. Glad we found out now–right? There's no way we can do this with everything going on, we just can't. Everybody sees it and so should we."

Jacob doesn't answer right back. "Yeah, right. Right." Zoe walks to the door alone and Jacob stays on the couch looking in a daze at the weed on his table. She unlocks the door then puts her hand on the doorknob, and he calls out to her. She answers as she opens the door. He says, "You know, if we leave one another it kind of makes us just like them. You know what I'm saying?"

She thinks about his words. "Yeah, I know. So, what should we do?"

He says, "For starters won't you come roll me one up." Jacob lifts a Backwoods package in his hand. Zoe thinks for a second then shuts the door; locks it back, then walks over to the couch to sit back down next to him.

Zoo

So, two weeks have passed. Ania is sitting down looking through a fortified fiberglass window at a gorilla outside in the sunlight sitting next to a batch of flowers, who is looking right back at her; that's when she hears Jill's voice.

"Oh, this is what we're doing today? This what we're doing?" She laughs. "The zoo, friend? We at the zoo, looking at gorillas, orangutans or whatever you call them along with assholes of zebras this morning?"

Ania stands up, and the friends hug and look around at their surroundings. “Girl, when you said you wanted to meet to catch up, I didn’t know we were going to be talking in front of this big ass, oversized monster. Damn how much do you think he weighs?” Jill has her eyes directly on the gorilla.

Ania says, “Girl, I don’t know, I’ve been coming here to see this damn gorilla since he was a baby.”

Puzzled Jill looks at her. “Why?”

“Because he doesn’t talk back, he just listens to my thoughts.”

Jill chuckles. “Yeah right, I need the name of your plug and some of what you’re smoking.”

“No, but for real, I like coming to the zoo. It’s just so peaceful.”

Jill looks at the gorilla again. “I guess, but I remember when I watched Cooley High with my daddy, he told me everything there is about gorillas.”

“Like what?”

“Like to never sit in front of a gorilla at the zoo, 'cause they will hit you with shit. Did you see that movie?”

“Yes, of course I saw it, it was a movie that wasn’t real,” Ania laughs.

“Well, if my daddy said, it was real, then damn it, it was real to me.”

Ania and Jill catch up on all the happenings because the last few weeks have gone by super-fast and they are both so delighted that Jacob is getting married and that’s one of the topics on their agenda.

Ania admits, "Yes, I can't believe my baby boy is getting married, isn't this a surprise. It's one thing to finally get the house to yourself, and to be able to walk around butt ass naked whenever you want. But to realize your son is getting married and tying the knot is a very big step that I hadn't even thought about because you know Jacob, he never did talk about marriage or anything."

"Well, yeah, he's a man. They're not going to talk about that until they are really ready to talk about it, even when they are married."

"You're not lying about that."

Jill says, "But damn to Lisa's daughter, though? How about that? It sounds like an Eric Jerome Dickey plot doesn't' it?"

Ania recalls, "Yes, and by the way, I miss his writing so much; GOD rest his soul." At the same time, their eyes venture over to the flowers under the beautiful sunshine. They share a thankful thought and smile of positive remembrance of their favorite author who gave them so much fun and joy with his work.

After a few minutes, Jill says, "But hey, I must admit, how do you feel about all this? Not only is Lisa going to be a part of your family, you two are going to cross paths one hell of a lot. You even have the engagement party tonight."

Ania says, "Wait a minute now, did you invite her or something, because I didn't."

Jill looks at Ania. "Girl, you know you have to invite her."

Ania says, "I didn't, but Jacob did; he called and said her name wasn't on the list, and he was adding it."

"You need to stop it," Jill says, "You're starting already."

"It's just so hard to believe she's been here all this time and Larenz didn't know. Doesn't that seem odd to you?"

"It does, but this is Atlanta, and I can see it happening because everything is so spread out."

"That's true, it could."

"So, have you thought about all the interaction you're going to have to have with her? You know there will be family functions, kids birthdays, anniversaries, all of that. How do you think you're going to react when she and Larenz speak, you know maybe get stuck in the kitchen together during Thanksgiving or something."

"You're trying to be funny, right?"

"No, I'm serious, it happens."

"Well, I don't know, if I hear her say something out of pocket or a crazy ass stare, I'm going to have to check her."

"Look at you– I think anything she says to him, you're going to be checking."

Ania says, "It's crazy, I didn't sign up for this."

"Yeah, you did, just didn't know this was in the fine print, baby, it will be okay."

"Well, those are the least of my problems right now."

"What do you mean?"

"I was talking to Larenz, and we were going at it a little, and I asked him if he would have married me if he knew that me and Bill had sex?"

"You did what?"

"Yes, I asked him that."

"Can I ask why?"

"Because, Nicole said to me that back in the day when I was supposedly going out with Bill, dating or whatever, we slept together, and Larenz knows about it. But Larenz and I talked about that before we left Chicago and for the first couple of years when we moved here, and he knows nothing happened. But she said that he knows, and it must have been difficult for him to take me back, and I guess it should give him a pass for the things that are happening now with Lisa showing up to the club; like she did and reading that funky ass poem."

"Damn after all these years, she brings that up?"

"Yes, and I don't know what to think of it. I mean we haven't even really sat down and talked about it since our conversation because I don't want to get into a back and forth with Nicole right now. She's just getting out of rehab and one thing the counselor said to me was to make sure her stress levels stay low, and that's exactly what I intend to do."

"Oh, you think she's back to the lying and storytelling she was doing years ago?"

"What else could it be because it's not true, and I love her like I love you, like a sister, and I don't want any drama."

Jill looks at Ania hard. "What? What is it?"

Jill says, "Well you know, I didn't grow up with all of y'all like that, and I have known you for a long time, not as long as the rest. But I can say Bill has a way of saying things insinuating that you two were quite an item."

"What?" Jill shakes her head yes. "Please."

"He is always saying little things. Bringing up how his act has a song that they want to sing, but he won't let them because it might offend Larenz."

"A song? What the hell?"

"Yeah, I don't know the name of it, I just ran up on them rehearsing it and caught some of the lyrics talking about, how hard it is to know that he made love to you or something or the other. I mean he was all into it and just swaying back and forth and when they were done they were like, so we're going to roll this out tonight, and he said no because of the reason I just told you about."

"Well, I don't know why Larenz would get mad 'cause he knows all we did was go out."

"Well, I don't know either, damn shame."

"Exactly," Ania says. They have a quick, quiet moment catching up to their thoughts. Ania is trying to understand what is really going on with Bill, then looks at Jill and follows her eyes. "Girl, what're you looking at?"

She says, "Ania, does this big ass gorilla, ape thing have a dick?"

"Girl, what?"

"A dick, where is it? I've been sitting in front of him all this time and ain't seen his dick yet?"

Ania looks at Jill, then at the animal. "I don't know, I mean he's so big it should be swinging somewhere down there, right?"

"That's what I mean, if I was a lady gorilla I wouldn't let something that big on top of me without a hammer, you heard me."

Ania laughs and takes a closer look at her friend. "I don't think he has one Jill." She stands up towards the glass and the gorilla stands. "Nope look, he doesn't have one, imagine that. Wow, I never knew?"

Jill takes her phone out. "That's some foolishness right there, his big ass has to have a dick. How do they make their babies? I'm going to look it up." Jill punches it up in her phone and starts to laugh as Ania is still standing looking at King Missing Dong. "Oh, my goodness," Jill says.

"What is it?"

"It says his thing is only one to two inches when it's fully erect and look he's bringing you a flower!" Jill can't stop laughing.

Ania turns around and looks out through the fiberglass window. "Oh, uh, uh you're lying to me." Then she looks closer as he holds the flower and puts it up to the glass. "I think I see his little thing right there; Jill, is that it?" Ania reaches into her bag and snatches her reading glasses and puts them on then takes another look. "Oh, my goodness, that's not good news at all, Jill. Is that all he has? He must have a fierce head game girl, ok... I mean out of this world because that right there is not the move."

Jill says, "Absolutely, his head game better be on point. This just ain't right friend; I tell you right now, it-is-not-right. Poor gorilla man, now I feel sorry for him. I don't remember my daddy telling me they had such itty-bitty ones."

Club

Tonight, Larenz is eager to get things back to normal working order in the club after Bill, and his beta act names come down from Club Nickels city landmark marquee. The club is packed and filled for the last performance, along with Jacob and Zoe's engagement party that Ania quickly put together, which seems low-key slick in Larenz's opinion. He hasn't brought up his perceived notions about the situation, things are still unstable with he and Ania, but he thinks it was done out of spite so that Lisa wouldn't beat her to it, and have the party at Marbles. Larenz is determined to stay ten toes down, and keep his opinion to himself. He and Ania are on speaking terms but they have yet to discuss the question she laid on him, about if he would have still married her if she would have slept with Bill. Larenz hasn't forgot about it; he put it in his mental rolodex because once Bill and his crew clears out, it will be better for everyone. He and Ania can sit down and talk about things like adults.

It's getting close for the night's festivities to begin with Bill's group performing, Kerry and Jill, and some poets on stage all night long with the club's DJ spinning sounds during the breaks. Larenz and JT are in the office, and Ania walks in, and lets him know that Calvin asked her to hand off a sealed manila envelope because he is on the phone with Cam and there are too many people coming in for him to leave the front door. When Larenz mentions to JT how good Ania looks, she looks back at him as she walks out the door; she doesn't say anything, only hums and purrs an acknowledgement. Larenz and JT laugh a bit and Larenz opens the envelope, counts the money and smiles. "Bop. We've done it again gotdamit," he says, as JT starts to clap his hands in celebration. "Three times as much as we predicted every night for an entire month. We're not going to have any problems with handling any situation that may come along to get the commercial completed. Yes, sir, good damn call my brother."

"Thank you very much good sir," JT tells him. "This is chess."

"Definitely not checkers. Look, don't let me forget, I'm throwing you some extra dollars off this. Let's just get the rest of the door, food, and drinks at the end of the night and tally up."

"Oh, I won't forget. You better believe that, and I appreciate you."

"No, my brother, I appreciate you."

There is a knock on the door. Larenz puts the envelope in his desk, then nods to JT; JT goes to the door, opens it. When they see that it's Calvin, JT goes back to his seat.

Calvin says, "Hey, I had to come back for a sec' because I just got off the phone with Cam."

JT looks over at Larenz wondering if they are going to have to make good on their promise to him. "Everything good?"

"Yeah, yeah all good. But Cam says the site manager down there told him, if he has to beg him to keep getting up on the scaffold he can't come back."

Larenz and JT smile. "Bruh, did Cam get your money back to you?" Larenz wants to know.

"Oh, yeah, he told me y'all rolled up on him."

JT says, "Yep and we should have."

"And will do it again, if need be," Larenz promises.

"No doubt," Calvin agrees. "Yeah, I got my money minus a few but he's been paying it back these last few weeks."

Larenz says, "Damn, okay, good. I didn't even ask him if he was scared of heights."

JT has an idea. "We can put him on the townhouse, they're landscaping that joint right now."

Larenz says, "He can work in the grass and dirt can't he?"

Calvin says, "Hell yeah, if he says he can't, I will be catching a case."

"Bet, I will text you the address to the townhouse to give to him," JT says.

Calvin says thanks, and tells them he needs to get back to the door and have someone walk the parking lot to make sure everything is cool. JT gets up, locks the door, then sits back down; he starts answering texts while Larenz pulls out the envelope, plops it on his desk, and then stares off in a daze.

JT says, "Yo, everything good?"

Larenz looks up to him. "Yeah man, just thinking about something Lisa told me when we had our little sit down. Dig, she was talking about how the men in her life have never shown any appreciation towards her."

"Bruh, you sure she just wasn't messing with your head? From what I can see she is fine and seems to have herself together."

"Look here, I'm talking like never in her life received a gift from a man."

"Not even from you when you were a young buck coming up?" Larenz tries to think back, and JT notices and helps him. "Not a bangle bracelet? Coach Bag? Necklace?" At every mention Larenz shakes his head no. "Bruh, what about a gotdam birthday card?"

Larenz is really trying to remember and pushes out his bottom lip while he slowly shakes his head back and forth. "Nah, nothing. I can't remember one thing. I do remember that we would go out dancing all the time."

"Dancing?"

"Yeah, man. I remember she likes to dance. We both did."

JT points to the money bag and looks around acting as though he is checking for Ania in an amusing way. "Well, what're you going to do, go buy her a gift with some of that money on your desk?"

They both laugh, "Nah man. I'm good on that. "But dig, take the gift aspect out of what I'm saying because that's not here nor there. But just imagine, being a woman in this world, the way this world operates for women and not ever, ever, receiving some type of material appreciation from a man who says he wants to be with you. That alone just blows me away. And it must be true because you just don't keep track of something like that, if you aren't hoping one day it could happen."

"Yeah, it's deep. But maybe she's the type who always isn't talking about material things. Things she likes and shit, I mean some women right away you know you have to buy them something to get anywhere. Now, that to me is a problem. No gift, no convo, definitely no loving," JT says.

Larenz looks at him. "Damn you out here trickin' like that JT?"

"Look, it's wild out here, has been for years, and you're not out here like me, trying to date. That's why I've been looking in to my poly thing, but that's another conversation. All I'm saying is, you can't know a female out here for a couple of hours before she is asking for something."

"Really?"

"Really. Nails, hair, money, they want to be on the payroll–my boy."

"All of them?"

"Put it like this, a lot of them. You know how they can't tell the good men from the bad?"

"Yeah?"

"Well, it's the same for us. We don't know who's out here paper chasing or trying to give good love, like Whitney used to sing."

Larenz says, "She told me something else, too."

"Like what?"

"Explained that she and Bill have been keeping in touch all these years and he always has my name in his mouth. Some low key, investigating on the sly, slick nonsense. Told me all this the night she did the poem on stage."

At the mention of Bill and the night Lisa came into the club and did the poem. JT has a sudden flashback. It was the very night he saw JT pull up in his car and walk towards the house. JT is thinking about bringing it up. He buried it from his memory because it would bring drama like he never knew. So, he vaguely hears Larenz ask him, as he rambles, that he noticed he called a few times that night. JT is nodding and bobbing his head as though he is fully engaged; he is at a mental standstill. He doesn't want to answer the question because he knows his answer could break up what has been damn near the epitome example of marriage he has ever seen. JT stands up and heads for the door, then tells him, "I was just checking on you bruh, when I called. C'mon let's go out here and enjoy this last night and have a good time."

JT waits for Larenz to lock the money up in the safe behind the Jean-Michel Basquiat painting in the office, and they are off to the main floor of Nickels to celebrate his son's engagement and last night of a very profitable business venture with Bill. They make their way through the club greeting friend's and guest with smile's.

"Damn, man, sometimes you just have to sit back, soak it all up, and enjoy what you've built," Larenz says. He looks around at the success of the night. The turnout is amazing, and everyone is having a good time.

JT tells him, "Damn right, and this is just a peek of what's happening, just wait until they get a look at the commercial building downtown. I dead ass, have a few more ideas for that joint, like making an entire black-owned business wing to help uplift and inspire."

Larenz gives JT a look. "I can see that."

"But guess what?"

"I'm listening."

"We don't even have to label it as black-owned. It's just business, you understand? We have to get past this black-owned this and that. We here, ain't going nowhere; we're making money, and we are doing business. To me, sometimes that phrase is hurting the progress. I'm inclined to think when you advertise your hard work as being black-owned, you have the majority run away from you along with a percentage of our own folk who won't support you either. Here's my thing, if it's a good product or service, then it's business in my book and we should move forward and build it brick-by-brick without the black-owned stamp. Let's just get it."

"I feel you," Larenz tells him. "That's especially true for big business." Larenz shouts over the music from the DJ. "Yo, on soul, let's just do it, put our people not just on a separate wing but sprinkle that beauty all through the building on every floor so examples will be made, this is Atlanta they already know what it is. And oh yeah, I almost forgot."

"What's good?"

"We're going to need a few offices set aside for black men, who have a business, are starting a business or who just want to come and vibe with other business owners to share and network."

"Exactly."

"After seeing how lost Cam has become, we can also use it to share some experiences with the youngins'. Our brothers need a safe place. Can't work from home isolated, no interaction with each other. We are going to change it up a bit and help brothers not only get on their feet but stand."

"No doubt." JT gives Larenz some dap.

"Now, pop that bottle, JT; let's get this night started my brother." They are at their table, and JT grabs a bottle out of the ice and nods over when he sees Ania, Jill and Nicole on their way over to join them. But first, the ladies see Jacob and Zoe sitting pretty next to the stage and stop to say hello. Larenz and JT smile as they already know tonight will be one for the books.

Greetings

Jacob introduces everyone to Zoe again, and they give her a hug and welcome her to the family.

"Nice to see you Mrs. Ways," Zoe says.

Ania grins ear to ear. "Wait a minute, we're 'gonna stop that Mrs. Ways right now. You're a part of my son's life, and my name is Ania today, tomorrow, and always to you, okay?" Ania gives Zoe a big hug.

Zoe says, "Okay, I'll remember. I have heard nothing but the best about you."

Ania has a quick pause. She doesn't know if Lisa has already given her opinion of what she thought of Ania, but she decides to keep things on a positive note. "I'm sure you have; my son hasn't said much because you know that's just how he is, but I knew he had someone on his mind for a long time and I'm finally happy to meet you and wish you both all the love in the world. Just remember one thing for me."

"I will, I promise."

"Just remember, marriage and love are give and take, but it's worth it you'll see." They hug again then Ania, turns to Jacob. "Jacob, she is so beautiful and warm baby, so far, so good."

"You think so ma?" Then he whispers in Ania's ear. "We kind of had our first disagreement but sat down and hashed it out, just like I watched you and dad do all these years. Could have gone another way for a moment. But, you see, we're here."

Ania grabs his hand. "Well baby, let me tell you, that is how you work things out. Sit down and discuss them, you two did right. Now, what y'all drinking over here and whatever it is, po-me-some."

–

Back at the table JT says, "Look at Ania; she is ready to have a good time tonight, over there getting ready to turn up with her baby boy."

"Yeah man, glad to see her happy. She's not been like herself around the house lately."

"Oh, word?"

"Yeah, not all the way. But it's all good though. We're about to have a good night. Everybody, you ready?"

"Of course, my boy, so ready that I invited my family tonight."

"Your family? We all the family you got with your lonely ass," Larenz jokes.

"Until tonight," JT tells him, then nods his head at the entrance where his guests are making their way past Calvin at the door. "I'm about to introduce you to new family members in a second or two."

"What're you talking' about?"

"Remember the poly situation I've been tossing around?"

"Yeah, I mean you ain't really been saying much, but yeah."

"Well, I'm not tossing any longer. I'm in a tribe now black man, and I think we're about to seal the deal, tonight."

"Tribe?"

"That's right." JT is looking at the ladies, and he can tell they are searching for him.

"So, tell me how that works with your tribe leading ass?" Larenz laughs.

"I ain't 'gotta tell you shit, just sit back and learn." JT gets up from the table. "Be right back bruh, with the fam…."

Larenz mumbles, "This guy." Then shakes his head and reaches for the bottle.

–

Larenz is at ease tonight, sitting at the table all alone. Calvin already let him know he has everything under control. He will make sure no one will hit the stage tonight, at least until the engagement party and Bill's act is complete since poetry is the staple of the club. He looks over at Ania and the ladies over at Jacobs table, and there seems to be some lively discussions taking place; Zoe seems to be right at home. JT has just finished hugging on female number two and looks like he is just giving them the rundown of the club; then the DJ fades the music down, and the lights on stage come up, and Jill and Kerry, with the rest of their band members are ready to put on a show. When the first note comes out of Jill's mouth everyone is just blown away. It sounds so soft, sweet, and raw with passion that it can't help but make everyone pay attention to every word she sings. Larenz is always amazed by her voice but tonight her first song is about love and he is staring over at Ania and the son they made together and as Jill sings tears start to form in his eyes and it feels as though he has done something right. After Jill and Kerry's set of five song's and a dedication to Jacob and Zoe, the lights on stage come up, and Bill appears, standing in front of them, holding the microphone, running his mouth and telling a few jokes.

Nicole is sitting next to Ania, she feels her phone vibrate. A package, she has been waiting on all day, was delivered to the guesthouse. She tells Ania, "Girl, I don't know if this is too much for me or not but I'm going to go back to the house and lay down for a few."

"You feeling okay?"

"Yes, I'm fine. I just don't want to do too much. We've been busy and my body is telling me to slow down," she says, "I already got a rideshare and will be home, and in my pajamas relaxing in no time."

"Are you sure, I can get someone to take you?"

"No, no, I'm fine." Nicole gives Ania, a hug tells everyone goodnight; and then heads toward the door. She hesitates for a few seconds, and laughs at one of Bills jokes as she exits.

–

Zoe turns to Jacob at their table.

"I wonder where my mother is? She told me she would be here by now."

Jacob is looking toward the stage and listening to Bill, and turns and says, "Did you text her?"

"Yeah, a bunch of times."

Jacob says, "Maybe something came up at the club? She'll be here. Trust me."

"I hope so," Zoe says. She picks up her phone and texts Lisa again. She doesn't know Lisa is sitting in her BMW in the parking lot of Nickels looking at all of Zoe's texts and listening to Erika Badu on her playlist. Lisa is at a stalemate, definitely conflicted about everything going on right now; the engagement, the new contact with Larenz and Ania, and the possibility of being alone once Zoe and Jacob get married, even more so than she is on day-to-day. After she gets another text from Zoe, she takes a deep breath, turns off the car, and decides to venture inside. She opens the car door, has another thought, then shuts the door, starts the car back up, and continues with her thoughts under Simple E's old school joint, "Play My Funk," bouncing through her car speakers.

Table Talk

Bill is right at home on stage.

"This has really been a treat to come from the West Coast to The A and vibe out with all of you, it really has. And I know that a few weeks ago, I mentioned I was working on signing Jill and Kerry. I just wanted to make it official and present them with a contract to come aboard my label, Vindictive Records, so that we can share their talent with the rest of the world." The crowd applauds, and Bill walks over to Kerry and Jill and hands them their contracts; then walks off stage and the DJ takes over and starts up some music to keep the vibe alive.

JT comes back to the table with a bottle from the bar. He starts to pour it in his glass then stops, turns the bottle upside down and takes a long ass hit then places it in front of him. "Whoa, I'm gonna' need all that tonight, plus sum," he says.

Larenz looks at him puzzled. "Negro, do you know what you're drinking? That's Sunset Rum. You're going to be knocked out sleep in a minute you keep drinking like that."

"I probably do need to go to sleep."

"What? And where did your girls go?"

"Girls?"

"That's what I said, the liquor hit you that hard all ready?"

"I heard what you said," he takes another swig, "But one of them; wasn't female."

"Say, what?"

"Just one of them. The other one used to be her husband but now is her best friend. He got that thang."

"What thang?"

"That operation, B, they're looking to link with another guy, but that guy ain't me."

"Are you serious?" Larenz looks out on the floor to see if he can catch a glimpse and JT tells him they have already left.

"Damn always something ain't it. I need a lady who really just wants to hold me down, it's crazy out here."

Larenz slightly points at him. "Wait, hold up. JT did I see you kiss them when they came in here?"

JT takes the bottle away from his lips, then wipes his mouth with the back of his hand. "What?"

"You heard me? Did you kiss them when you greeted them?"

"Nah, nah I hugged them."

Larenz is enjoying his messy moment. "I don't know my boy: I think you kissed them I'm gonna' have to roll back the security tape. Let me check the time so I can get right to it." Larenz looks at his watch.

JT thinks for a minute. "I did just hug them right?" Larenz puts his hands up letting him know he wasn't sure. "Bruh, this stays between us. You got it? And damn that tape."

"Yeah, man, just messing with your poly ass. I got it."

"They could have told me that from the jump. I told you bruh, It's not fair out here." JT takes the bottle and turns it up again. "Got me fucked up," he declares.

Larenz gets a good twenty minutes or so to calm JT down while putting more drink in his system and getting him to realize it could have gone another way. Although JT is heated, Larenz reasons with him and helps him to rationalize it's for the better that he found out like he did. It isn't long after that their table has become packed with guests. Ania, Jill, Kerry and JT with Calvin coming back and forth making sure everybody is good with enough food and drink to celebrate the night. GOD only knows how they got on the conversation. But they are sitting around chatting it up about one of their favorite topics that they have yet to resolve and probably never will.

"Well, I don't know who you can really classify as the best female singer of all time. There are so many. Now, I as a singer have favorites because they're all so unique to me and they make me a fan. I focus on tone, delivery, pitch, lyrics and sound; it's all beautiful every last voice. Minnie Riperton, Patti Labelle, Macy Gray with her raspy flow, Randy Crawford, Anita Baker, Stephanie Mills, my girl Lalah Hathaway, Jill Scott and Nina Simone there are so many.

Larenz jumps right in. "Check this out Jill. I agree they're all nice, but Phyllis Hyman will always be at the top of my list. Her *Living All Alone* album will take you someplace you've never been every time you spin it, ya dig."

"And y'all know about his album collection?" Ania brags a bit. "You can always find her at the ready next to the turn table."

Larenz places his hand over his heart and says, "No doubt, forever. And I will tell you this Rachelle Ferrell gets much play too."

Ania says, "Well, let's not sit here and not put Tina Marie's voice in this discussion cause Ms. Thang would light it up and listen to this, there was no difference in her voice whether in concert or on wax, BaeBae; she was what she was all the time."

Kerry steps in it, "Now, y'all know I don't say much. I usually just soak all of your greatness up and use it to create. But the first three female artists I met coming up, I have always been partial to." He takes a second just to shake his head. "Angela Bofill, Chante' Moore and my baby sitting right here Jill. It just doesn't get better than that for me." Everyone sitting around the table put their opinions to his choices and then Bill walks over right before Ania is about to start their next round of conversation on music; of who actually has the best record between Glenn Jones, Howard Hewett and Lillo Thomas in their songs, all named "Show Me," which would have them debating for hours.

Bill finds a spot and looks around the table. "What's good? Everybody good? This has turned out to be a wonderful joint venture Larenz. It really has. We might have to do this again sometime. All the reviews we're getting is nothing but love and I have my team attacking social and getting the word out. Damn, if momentum keeps up like this, I'm going to have another number one on my hands soon enough." Bill looks over at Larenz.

"Yeah, glad we could help out. He nods over to Jill and Kerry and smiles. Just make sure you take care of my people right here. I need you to make sure their sound stays sweet as they create it."

Bill is very sarcastic with a smile on his face, "Oh, yeah. As soon as I can get them to sign." Then everyone at the table laughs.

Kerry pats on his suit jacket. "Got it right here, just need to get my people to take a look at it. You know this is music and business."

Bill agrees with him, then looks over at Ania in a different kind of way. Trying to be smooth and all suave. "So, how are you Ania? Enjoying the night?"

Ania is already buzzing, and she is quick and short. "Fine Bill thanks."

"That's good," he looks around. "I saw Nicole leave she good?"

Ania says, "Just a little tired, that's all."

"I hear that, soon as we're done here, I'm off to Monaco for a minute to recharge, you know what I mean?" Bill gives Ania a look, and Larenz and JT notice. Everyone does especially Ania. Larenz remembers that creepy ass look; it's just like the one he tried to shoot at Ania on the sly back in the day. His comment hits JT differently because Larenz is his boy, and he can feel the heat inside of his body quickly turning into a way Bill won't understand if he doesn't shut his big mouth.

Hexed

When Nicole gets back to the guest house a package is waiting for her at the front door; and she scoops it up, opens the door, then places it on Ania's favorite table. Nicole hustles back into her bedroom and comes out in her housecoat, slippers with a pair of scissors in her hand. She fights off the urge to rip the package open; she sits it down and takes a few deep breaths before she starts at the sides with the scissors to get to what's inside. She has been waiting all day even has called the shipping company to assure the package was on the way. She finally gets the first layer of the package open, then laughs at the fact she is going to have to get through some wrap and more plastic to get to it. When she finally opens it all the way, Nicole grabs what she has been waiting on; she stands up and lets it drape down to the floor. She says out loud, "Oh, my goodness, it's beautiful. Just like you said it would be. I didn't know at first what to think when you asked me to marry you, but I guess it's cool; I mean, I have never been married, so let's do this." She turns her wedding dress around in her hands, kicks off her slippers, takes off her housecoat, and puts the dress on. Nicole is feeling so good. She didn't know what type of feeling the dress would bring over her, but it is better than anything she could imagine. She walks with it on and goes toward the mirror on the wall in the bedroom. She stands for a while, looking at herself, and her eyes began to well up; she smiles. Her eyes suddenly tighten as though she is listening and she responds. "Yes, of course I'll meet you down at the court house. It's okay if we don't have a big wedding. I just want us to be happy and with one another forever. Give me about twenty-minutes, and I'll be there, just make sure you're there."

Nicole goes into her closet, picks out a pair of shoes, and places them in her bag. She puts on her sneakers as she talks herself into walking to the court house instead of waiting on a ride. When she is ready, she grabs her coat and is out the door. It's a little chilly outside, but she stands in front of the main house and decides to go down the street towards downtown. To get to the main thoroughfare, she has to walk down a winding road. Ten minutes into her travels, she can feel a car following her in the darkness, but she does not turn around. The car doesn't pass it just continues to follow. Soon after she hears a police siren and an officer on a speaker telling her to stop and turn around. Nicole turns around, sees the police, and is terrified; then starts to run away.

On the Mic

Lisa is in the car and cannot in good conscience continue to not answer Zoe's calls and texts. She knows she needs to go in and pay her respects, but just doesn't want all the attention coming at her like– there's the crazy bitch who owns the club crosstown, that did the poem and moved from Chicago to Atlanta to stalk Larenz. But she has no excuse not to be there. So, she shuts off her car and ventures inside to support Zoe and Jacob.

Inside the club, for the past few minutes, Bill's ass has been saying slick nonsense around the table. Basically, he is flexing about his life and what he has done over the years; no one was paying attention because it is being said to make everyone else feel as though they hadn't accomplished anything and weren't on his level. But that is where he is wrong; everyone at the table has first-hand knowledge on how he moves and is looking at him like he is a damn clown. He doesn't even know it, which shows everybody that what they were thinking about him is true.

As he sucks the vibe from the table, Ania has her head turned in another direction because the madness is thick. For a time, she removes herself from the table and dances with Jacob and Zoe. When she returns, Bill is still talking nonstop, which she does not care to hear. She did find the time to text Nicole, but she doesn't answer. Ania is sure by now she is already snuggled up and sleeping. Calvin comes to the table again to make sure everyone is okay.

Ania calls out to him and says, "Calvin can you bring out another bottle please?"

It takes Bill about half a second to open his mouth. "Just like the old days, trying to get that drink up in ya'. I remember those days very well." He smiles.

It gets awkward very quick, and Ania notices Larenz trying to fight through his uneasiness. She finishes whatever she has in her glass and says, "Don't even try it. All your embellishments are getting tired."

Bill looks around at everyone before he speaks. "Embellishments? My memory is game tight," he says. "I remember everything, and everybody I do it with, and I do mean everything," he boasts. There are a few moans and groans around the table and some glasses are put down on the table in a hurry because of the slick garbage running out of his mouth.

JT is ready for such a moment; and he already has his arm across Larenz's chest, so he can't get out of his chair and throw hands. JT says, "I think you need to excuse yourself."

"C'mon now, let's enjoy this last night together. Ain't no secret me and Ania used to kick it; I mean, we all grown now. We done got over all that teenybopper shit, right?"

Ania jumps in. "Negro please, I went out with you a handful of times, that is not kicking it."

Bill pauses and looks around the table and stops at Larenz. "I remember different."

Larenz says, "Look here Bill, you were already told to leave the table. So, what're you going to do, 'cause it can get done for you."

He looks at Larenz, then JT, and everyone else with his smug ass smile. "Okay, no problem, no problem at all." He raises up, smooths out his shirt, gives everyone a look, and moves along.

The table is quiet for a moment.

"Punk ass…"Ania says.

Larenz can feel everyone's eyes on him as he stares at the remainder of the yac in his glass. He thinks for a minute and then says, "Kerry let me holler at you." He stands a few feet from the table, and Kerry walks over.

Jill says, "Damn, it doesn't take long to figure people out does it?"

"No, I've been telling you girl, he's a complete idiot. Has always been and never will change," Ania says.

JT chimes in, "But does he know how close he was to getting that ass beat? As long as we've been in this club, we ain't never come that close to fuckin' somebody up in here. I'm talking, throwing his ass on top of this table and beating some respect back up in him." JT looks around to see exactly where Bill ventured to. He sees him over across the club, talking to a few ladies and ordering drinks. JT's eyes are tight, and he is definitely ready to put in work if need be; because he is still uptight about his poly situation gone bad.

Jill says, "It must be years of pent-up animosity searing in his soul. It's like he pokes to provoke. I'm glad y'all didn't let him get a response out of you. But I know you wanted too."

JT picks up the bottle of drink as soon as Calvin sits it on the table. "Forget him. We're celebrating tonight. Let's get into this."

Ania says, "Yes, let's."

The table is calm for a second and everyone's trying to get their manners intact from almost being a part of the dust up and are looking out into the club. And it's like everyone sees Lisa at once walk through the door, stop, look around, and then go over to Jacob and Zoe's table.

JT looks at Ania. "You cool?"

She tells him she is.

Jill overhears him. "Of course, she is. Pour us some drink JT."

"My pleasure ladies." JT is filling up all the glasses, notices Larenz glass but turns and doesn't see Larenz or Kerry; seconds later, the lights in the club dim and then come back up and Larenz's ass is up on stage. JT says, "Would you look at this? This man ain't been up there in a while, awwww shit. He must have something to say." Then the snare drum is heard throughout and everyone knows there is a poet on stage. When the club realizes it's Larenz they greet him with so much love and he smiles and accepts every bit of it because he needs it more than they know.

"Thank y'all. Thank you so much. You know I haven't been on the mic for a minute, but you know, sometimes things present themselves, and when you are a creative, it's just so difficult to let it pass. So, can you bear with me for a minute? Because this is just off the top of my dome tonight." The crowd gives Larenz their approval, and he hears words of encouragement throughout. When he is ready, he nods over at Kerry along with the musicians on stage; they start in on a nice mellow beat that grabs everyone's attention right away. Larenz stands and receives the flow of the beat then takes it away.

After his poem Larenz pauses and smiles and asks, "Family–y'all alright?" As usual, in Larenz Ways fashion, he takes a slow downward bow, places his hand on his heart, and walks off stage.

–

Larenz gets back to the table and JT is all in. "Say, no more, my brother. I felt that smack way over here– yes sir!" Then he hands Larenz a glass to drink and picks up the bucket of ice on the table. "Here, put your hand in there it will take the swelling down."

Larenz dismisses JT with a smile and some dap.

Jill says, "I see somebody still has his chops, go'head Larenz with your bad self."

Ania looks at him lovingly, shakes her head, and smiles even though they still have a few things to sort out.

Larenz takes a sip of his drink. "Had to get a few things off my chest, that's all, ya dig?"

JT has his eyes on incoming, and he stops pouring his drink. As soon as he sits down the bottle, Bill is back, standing over the table looking at Larenz and opens his mouth. "Look, if I didn't know any better I would think you were talking about me in your little limerick."

Larenz is not holding back his mouth anymore. "If the topic matter makes you feel some kind of way, then so be it, Bill, you know, sometimes it just be like that."

Bill moves a little closer to Larenz but Larenz doesn't

flinch one bit. "Look, I know you might be in a bad situation with your girl because I'm here and a part of her past. But ain't no need to put it on stage like that nigga. I mean gotdamn what is the deal? You still holding on to the past or what?"

"Holding on to what? You ain't been a thought in my mind. Believe that, matter of fact me and mine been getting along quite nicely before you ever stepped in my club to upgrade your shit by using my shit."

Bill looks around. "You're right. You right. I asked."

Larenz says, "So, here's the deal. It is what I said, so move on."

Bill is silent, but Ania has had enough. "No, look this is not the place to have this conversation. Bill since you like to walk around and give your little innuendoes about me. Why don't we all go back to the office and settle this once and for all. I'm tired of your mouth and I'm not going to live the rest of my life with you walking around talking crap about me. Let's straighten this out tonight."

Bill says, "Look, I'm willing to do whatever you like."

"Let's go to the office Larenz to clear this up." Ania turns to Larenz when he doesn't say a word as he peers at Bill. "Can we go in your office Larenz? We are clearing this up right now."

The back and forth at the table is not loud and belligerent enough to draw attention to those enjoying themselves inside. But Jacob has a keen sense and can tell something over at his parents' table isn't going as smoothly as possible, and lets Zoe and Lisa know that he'll be right back which gives them a chance to talk.

–

Zoe scoots closer to her mom and says, "Glad you were finally able to make it."

"You know I wouldn't miss this for the world."

"I certainly hope not. I was five minutes away from leaving to come check on you to make sure you were okay?"

"Of course, I am baby just had some things to work through." She notices the look Zoe gives her of not understanding her completely. "I don't know. Just some thoughts of you as a little girl, growing up, graduating college and now about to get married. You know, good thoughts."

"Aww, that's so nice."

Then Lisa says, "And also wondering how much time you'll be spending here instead of what we built across town?"

Zoe smiles then says, "Ma, don't start. You know how we do it on the other side of town. I'm still committed to make Marbles the best spot in the city."

"Well, that's nice to hear."

"C'mon, you know it's what we do. Hey listen, Jacob always told me that Larenz was a beast on the mic, but seeing him in person, my goodness. He's fantastic– right?"

"Yes, he's definitely a word slinger that's for sure." Lisa looks down.

"Ma, you okay?"

"Yeah baby, this is just all too much, that's all. It's a lot to take in– seeing a few people from my past." Zoe agrees by nodding. "If you don't mind, I'm going to head back to the club. If you didn't know, we're pretty packed over there too."

"Of course," Zoe says, "I'm just glad you stopped by. Me and Jacob will swing-by and help you with the close."

Lisa smiles and grabs Zoe's hand. "I'm proud of you baby. So happy for you."

"Thanks ma, I know this isn't very comfortable for you. But we will work it out. I promise you that."

True or Not

Jacob walks up to JT, who is standing on the outside of Larenz's office door, and he daps JT up. "Yo', what's going on? Everything good JT?"

"Yeah, young blood all good, they just inside hashing out some issues that's all."

"Issues?' Who's inside?"

"Your mom, pops and Bill."

"What kind of issues?"

"Not my place, I'm just here 'cause I always am, you know that."

Jacob looks at JT, then at the door but doesn't move; and can hear voices, but can't hear what's going on inside.

–

Bill is sitting across from Larenz at his desk and Ania is standing next to Larenz. Bill has a mocking look on his face almost as though he feels they look like Prince Akeem Joffer's parents on their throne. But Ania has been drinking all night, her buzz is correct and she wants the bad vibes off of her name.

Bill rubs his hands together. "Okay, we're here, what do you want to talk about?"

"Oh, this is a quick discussion," Ania tells him. "You're trying to ruin my reputation with my friends; I don't even know if you already have done so."

Bill says, "I don't know what you're talking about. I don't have anything but love for you and Larenz."

Ania says, "Oh, really now?"

"It's the truth."

"Is it the truth that you told Nicole that you and I had sex?"

Bill thinks her words are comical. "Nicole? Nicole? You are coming to me with something Nicole has said? If, I'm wrong stop me, but didn't she just get out of a mental facility? You don't have to answer because I know the answer to that question because I'm the one who paid for her stay in that muthafucka."

Ania is not amused. "There are others, too."

"Like Lisa," Larenz shoots out.

"Lisa?"

"That's right."

"So, after all these years you still care what she talkin' about L?" Bill shrugs his shoulders, twists his lips, and looks at Ania.

Ania's eyes travel down to Larenz.

"Hell nah, don't try to deflect. The point of it all is you're throwing shade out in the streets Bill."

"Not my game L."

Larenz says, "You're lying."

"Well, we can just straighten this all out right now," Ania says.

Bill says, "Yes, please let's do that."

"Okay, so Larenz knows a long, long time ago, when we were younger we went out for a matter of weeks."

Bill has a crooked look on his face, and is staring directly at Larenz. "That's right."

"So, within that short time, I want you to tell me in front of my husband when and where we supposedly had sex like everyone believes?"

Bill doesn't answer right away. There is just a long-extended pause, so much that he and Larenz are able to lock eyes. Then Bill moves his eyes towards Ania, as though they share the same long kept secret before he exhales; then he stands. "A gentleman never tells you know that."

Larenz raises up from his chair and he is so loud, that JT and

Jacob can hear outside the door. "What the hell is that supposed to mean? You either did or you didn't?"

Bill still has the half smile on his face like he has one upped the situation again. "It means what it means."

No one has to tell JT to come into the office because he already has and Jacob is standing right beside him. "We good in here?" JT wants to know.

Bill turns around and looks in the doorway. "Yeah, we Gucci –or whatever the hell y'all say in The A? I was just on my way out the door."

Ania says, "Yeah, you need to get your lying ass outta' here Bill, did you want me that bad that you have to lie about it after all these years?"

Larenz says, "Look you lying on my wife nigga, you better watch yourself out here."

As Bill walks away he turns around, "That makes two of us," he tells Larenz, and JT nudges him out the office.

-

Larenz assures JT and Jacob that he is cool and wants to be alone with Ania. After they leave, he sits without a word in his chair, wondering what is going on.

"Larenz, Bill is lying out his gotdam mouth," Ania tells him. "I can't believe we're back to this after what seems a lifetime."

"Yeah, well, maybe somethings in the dark need to come to light."

Ania looks at him. "What do you mean by that?"

"I'm just saying right now, I don't know what to believe. This man rides into town and has been talking smack all these years, holding on to the words he's saying like they are the gospel."

"Well, he's lying."

"Why would he lie? That's what I want to know? What is the payoff?"

"So, you believe him, don't you?"

"I didn't say that but all I know is he didn't say no and weeks ago you ask me a question whether I would have married you– if I knew that he did and I am not supposed to think about it?"

Ania is speechless she doesn't have a response and walks over to her purse on the couch to answer her phone as Larenz looks on. "Oh, my goodness," she says.

"What's happening?"

"It's Nicole she's been picked up by the police. I need to see what's going on."

Believe Him?

JT is now back sitting at the table with Jill, Kerry and Jacob. He notices Ania coming out of the office. The entire night is turning out to be nothing but drama, and topping it off, Jill and Kerry huddle up and discuss Bill and his antics. They are definitely thinking about telling him to kiss their ass. Even though the club is still packed, Bill's act has finished for the night, the DJ has taken over all the sounds, and JT lets Bill know before he leaves that he owes them one more check. The club has mellowed out, and for the last hour or so Calvin opens up the stage for some poetry. Everyone is in a chill mode.

JT makes his way back into the office. Larenz is sitting there staring at his glass of yac. "Yo you good?"

Larenz looks up. "Yeah, thanks, JT."

JT notices the anxiety on his face. "No, you're not. It's okay to say you're not because for me I think this whole situation is tired."

"Yeah? You think so?"

"Yes, I do, just the instant drama someone can bring into your life for no reason. Bro that fool is so lucky we have grown over the years. Back in the day it would have meant nothing to put hands on him."

"I tried to tell you it's what he's always done, it's who he is."

"Well, I caught a bit of what he was saying. You believe him?"

"I don't know. And the way that I'm feeling now makes me recall a lot of things that I placed away in the memory bank and I can really say if I knew he did do anything with Ania I can truthfully say I wouldn't have married her. That's how bad this guy irked me back in the day, and if I find out that she let that type of energy in her space, it's a wrap, no questions."

"Well, Ania is denying it so what are you going to do?"

"I don't know, I mean what can I do? I never even thought of doing anything different than always being with her." JT sits silently, thinking to himself, and unconsciously shakes his head. Larenz sees him. "What? What is it?"

"Look, I have something to tell you. The night you asked me to take Ania home when Lisa came in and did that poem... when I was leaving, there was a car pulling up to the house. I looked into it, and I saw, Bill."

"Bill?"

"Yeah man, he drove right past me. I parked the car waited for him, just to double check, and it was him."

"You didn't tell me, you just now telling me JT?"

"Yeah, I'm just now telling you. You and Ania are my hero's, black man. You two have been together longer than anyone I have ever known in my life, including my parents, grandparents my whole got damn family tree. I didn't want to be the one to tell you no shit like this. But I saw him and I just had to."

–

Now, it's damn near three in the morning Larenz is still at the club, and JT comes in the office. "You good?" Larenz nods yes. "Talk to Ania yet?"

"Yeah, and I straight up asked her if Bill was over and

she's denying it."

JT shakes his head. "Look, I got nothing but love for Ania; and her not being upfront with you makes me a liar. And I know what I saw. But hey, my mama always told me that females will take things to their graves rather than telling the truth." Larenz thinks about his words. "Look, let me take you home."

"No, I'm good. I'll stay here."

"You sure?"

"Yeah, I think it's best; plus, Nicole has a situation and Ania went up to the facility and is sitting up there trying to find out what's going on."

"Aight, call me if you need anything. Everything is locked up," JT lets him know before he walks out.

Larenz sits back onto his couch and finally gets to think about the upper-cut JT hit him with in silence. At first, Larenz tries to blame himself because it is the same night he was over at Lisa's but his mind clears up, and he remembers that he told Ania about being there the next morning. In his mind it was the perfect time to tell him about seeing Bill. It is so hard for Larenz to be sympathetic and upset at the same time. Ania doesn't understand what is going on with Nicole and he respects that even though their personal relationship is a mess, he genuinely wants to be there for her. But the energy of their situation is keeping him away. His emotions are tumbling and all the thoughts running through his head are not all good ones. Some of his thoughts have bad intentions and he knows he needs to think all of his actions out because it is what he has always done; so, he decides to sit tight; that's until his phone rings and he answers.

"Larenz?"

"Lisa?"

"Yes, are you doin' okay? I understand you had one hell of a night?"

"Yeah, I did. I guess since we're going to be really family soon you will know these types of things about me, right?"

"I guess. Maybe we'll know them about each other."

He says, "Right, you're right, but I'm cool."

"Well, I just want you to know when I told you that if you ever needed a friend, I would be here for you, and I am."

"Thanks, I really appreciate that."

She pauses. "Well, I know that the sun will be up in a few hours but if you want to come over, you're welcome."

"Thank you, I'll keep that in mind."

"You do that. I just sent over the address in text. Take care."

Larenz checks his phone, and just like she said she would, Lisa sends him her address. Larenz gets up off the couch and he has so much on his mind that he starts to walk around the inside of his club. For over an hour, he walks around the club thinking about everything going on and at one time finds himself standing on stage just looking out into the darkness because it is exactly where he feels he is, at the moment. He grabs the microphone stand, closes his eyes, and opens them as though he has an idea. He rushes to his office grabs his keys and phone. On the way to his car through the darkness of the parking lot, he is unaware Bill is standing nearby, watching every move he makes.

–

Ania doesn't make it home until almost noon after spending the entire night with Nicole. It is a relief that Nicole is okay and that her doctor at the facility wants to keep her for a few days to make sure she doesn't have another episode. When Ania gets in the house she sees no signs of Larenz not even any indication that he has been home since last night. She calls his phone, and there is no answer; it goes straight to voicemail. She calls JT and asks if Larenz is with him.

JT is baffled; she hasn't heard from Larenz. "Uhh, no, he told me he was staying at the club for the night."

Ania says, "That's funny because I just talked to Calvin he told me Larenz is not there and his car is not in the parking lot."

"Yeah, that is strange. I left him and he was sitting in his office on the couch."

"Was he alone?"

"Yeah, all by himself."

"He didn't call or text you this morning?"

JT looks through his phone. "Uhh, no text or calls."

"Strange."

"Look, this doesn't sound like Larenz. Long as I have known him I've always been able to reach him. Let me make some calls and see what I can find out."

"Call me back JT… okay?"

"I got you."

Ania tries to get a quick nap. She is very tired from being up all night. But now not knowing where Larenz could be is only adding more stress. She picks up her phone and dials his number and still it goes to voicemail. Then she tries to remember if there was anything he told her that he needed to do, but she comes up blank and automatically starts to think if he could be so stupid to go over Lisa's because he is mad at her for Bill's absurd claims. Ania isn't going to sit around and wait for an answer; she changes clothes and goes over to the only place she knew Lisa would possibly be to find out, if in fact she has seen Larenz.

–

It's close to two in the afternoon and Ania pulls into the parking lot of Marbles and she doesn't have to even go inside the club because she notices Lisa getting out of her car. Ania pulls up right beside her and gets out of her car.

Lisa is surprised. "Ania?"

"Lisa."

They both take a few seconds to scan the other. "Can I help you with something?"

Ania is quick. "I'm looking for Larenz. Have you seen him?"

Lisa's facial expression is dismissive. "No, I haven't."

Ania doesn't want to say but does anyway, "Well, he didn't come home last night and I haven't heard from him."

Lisa looks her up and down. "Well, I can't really blame him."

"Excuse me?"

"Just sayin' Ania, the way I hear you and Bill been moving all these years keeping secrets."

"Look, I don't know what you're talking about. I'm damn sure not talking about Bill with you. I just want to know if you have seen Larenz?"

"Didn't I already tell you no?"

Ania turns away to get back into her car. Before she gets in, Lisa says, "I did talk to him though."

Ania turns around. "Why didn't you just say that? When?"

"'You asked if I'd seen him, last night. It was early this morning around three that we spoke."

"Three?"

"Yes, I told him he could come over to talk if he needed to."

"Oh, really?"

"But he was out of it. He didn't say he wouldn't, but I sent him my address, and he didn't come by."

Ania gives her a long stare and then gets into the car and drives away.

–

Ania calls JT and relays the information Lisa gave to her. JT hangs up and knows damn good well; this is not Larenz. As long as he has known him there has never been a day they were not in touch even on vacation. JT doesn't want to think the worse, but it isn't like Atlanta's crime isn't sky high and damn near out of control. So, it gives him pause and he wants to start looking for his brother right away. There were already a few police officers that would work security at the club, so JT calls in a favor. He let them know that his boy was missing and asked if they could get some guys to be on the lookout. JT waits a few more hours to find out if there is any word, and when he doesn't get any information he calls Calvin, Cam, Kerry and Jacob to the club to let them know what is going on. They are all sitting at the bar.

"Look, there is no easy way to say this," JT says. "Now I already talked to Jacob, but I wanted everyone to know that nobody has seen Larenz since last night after close; to be exact."

"What the fuck, JT? What do you mean?" Calvin wants to know. "Larenz don't go missing, man that's not even him."

"That's why I'm calling this meeting because I feel the same way."

Kerry says, "Where could he be? Where was he going?"

"That's what I don't know. I left here, made sure the place was locked up, and he said he was staying the night on the couch. Nobody has heard from him since."

The youngest at the bar chimes in "So, what you want us to do Unc?"

"I was going to close the club tonight, but I think it's best if we stay open and keep our eyes and ears open to anybody mentioning they have seen Larenz."

"And Cam, I know how you have your ears to the street, so we need to find out if the streets are talking."

Cam says, "I can do that."

Jacob stands up. "Look, this my pops out here. I have text and called and haven't received a response yet. Something is not right. Not only do I need your help, but your prayers too." Everyone is in agreement and is on board trying to locate Larenz.

–

About two hours later, Bill comes strolling into the club and JT looks at him very oddly.

"What's good JT?"

"You tell me?"

"Just came by to chat with Larenz."

"Is that right? Bout what?"

"Need to square things up with him. Make sure we cool and all."

"And how are you going to do that because you could have done that last night?"

"Yeah man, I just answered the best way I could. You can understand that right?"

"Nah, I can't because I ain't never went behind my boy's back to get to his lady no matter how young y'all were back in the day."

"I respect that. But check this out. Just respect my answer, I gave to him and that's what I want to say to Larenz."

"Look, he's not here at the moment, so it's going to have to wait. I don't think he wants to hear that bullshit anyway."

"Well, I will just have to wait and see won't I?"

"Is that all Bill?"

"Look, if you ever see Larenz again let him know I stopped by." He turns around and starts to walk away.

JT is in his face before he takes two steps. "What the hell you just say to me?"

"What's wrong JT is there a problem with what I said?"

JT can't get any closer to Bill. He wants to grab him by his neck and bounce his head against the bar. But he manages to get through his emotions because he doesn't really know if Bill even knows Larenz is missing, but he knows for sure his mouth is about to get him fucked up. He takes a deep breath. "Get the fuck 'outta here." Bill steps away and mumbles something about anger issues under his breath.

Tell it

Ania is definitely going through it and Jill convinces her that she is going to hang out with her all day because she needs support and that's what friends do. Ania was sure the last time she went to the facility it would be her last and when they get out the car to walk inside she looks at that old worn out, wearied looking park bench that Nicole is so enamored with and cut her eyes away from it quickly.

"Thank y'all for coming to see me," Nicole says. She has on a facility gown, and the wedding dress she had on is hanging up, all alone in the closet. Ania can't take her eyes off of it because it is her first time seeing it.

"Girl, you scared me half-to-death." Jill agrees with Ania. "Are you sure you're okay?"

Nicole smiles, "I'm fine, it was nice seeing your face last night when I woke up, and now both of you are here. I feel much better."

Jill says, "You know we are here for you."

Ania says, "No worries whatsoever. Let's just get you better and back home."

"Well, it seems you have enough to worry about right now, other than me," Nicole says. Jill rubs Ania's folded hands as tears flow down her face for about the tenth time since they have been together.

"I'm going to be fine, and Larenz is fine too. I feel like he's fine, I really do," she tells them. "But I just want to hear his voice. Just one time, that's all I want."

Nicole and Jill can't take to hear Ania's broken heart coming through her voice, and the moment is about to take them all down into tears until they hear someone walk in the room then suddenly stop.

Nicole looks over and says, "Lisa? Lisa is that you?"

Lisa stands still when she sees Ania and Jill in the room, then waves her arm, which is about waist high. "Yes, hey, hi," she says almost like she wants to kick herself for interrupting. "I'm so sorry, I disturbed you all, I heard you were here and wanted to check in on you. I'm sorry again."

Ania can't take her eyes off Lisa and doesn't speak to her even after Jill says hello.

Nicole says, "It's okay; come on in, sis. It is so good to see you after all these years."

Ania sighs.

Lisa pushes herself in and she keeps looking at Ania.

Nicole has a thought, "Wait a minute, how'd you know I was here?"

Lisa groans, "Bill." Everyone in the room isn't surprised and comments about his nosey-always-in-their-business ass, and then they become silent; it's awkward because there is definitely friction and negative energy between Ania and Lisa.

Nicole says, "Now I know you two ain't still mean mugging after all these years?"

Ania says, "Yeah something like that. She still wants my man, after all these years, that's what it is."

"Actually, I don't, and he wouldn't if he was forced to leave you. He loves you, so get over me."

Nicole interrupts them. "Hold on ladies, see this is what got me in here like this. The same thing you ladies are doing. Thinking I knew something and in reality I didn't know a damn thing. You know a lot of times sisters; we bring heartache to ourselves. We fight, disagree, and hate each other, over a man. Not saying, Larenz isn't a good man, and we pray to GOD we hear from him soon. But one thing I learned, when I was tucked away all alone and allowed myself to forget that quick, is that we are damn good women and should stick together and talk things out when they need to be discussed for our own mental health and peace. Y'all don't know, but Bill has been telling me he wants to marry me for years."

"What?" Ania says.

Lisa says, "Really?" Right after Jill mentions he is really a messy man.

Nicole looks at Ania and says, "Yes, girl, and you don't know because I didn't tell you, and just kept listening to his bullshit until my mind just blanked out. You know there is no way I wanted to be back up in here, but one thing we all should know is that this muthafuka, Bill isn't good for any of us. He doesn't deserve our love or friendship. Now, I want everyone in here to grab hands, and we are going to say this prayer of sisterhood and talk out what you two have going on. Then I'm going to tell you everything that's been going on with my crazy ass and that nigga, and we're going to leave it here." They all laugh and agree. "Now c'mon grab hands."

Get Away

Later, the same day in Chicago, Isaiah says, "Enough with the pleasantries, black man. Now, I know for damn sure you didn't leave everyone you love; hop on no red-eye to come way out here to get a massage with my black ass. And on top of that, you didn't tell anybody where the hell you went?"

"Exactly what I did. It's trouble in paradise," Larenz tells him.

"So, what did you do? What is it? Some twenty-something year-old itch? Have you realized your best days are behind you, and you're looking for something, but you don't know what it is? Because if that's the case…"

"Nah, nah slow down. Nothing like that. It's Ania."

"Ania? She okay?"

"Yeah, but like I told you, Bill's ass done slid into town. Talking slick to everybody we know and bringing back old wounds and scars that we done forgot about."

"Like what?"

"Fucking my wife before I married her, that's what."

"Wait, what?"

"And that ain't all."

"Tell me, what else?"

"JT told me he saw his ass creeping to my spot when I wasn't there."

"At your house?"

"At, my, house."

"At your house and you ain't there?"

"That's right. So, if I would have stayed in Atlanta I would be in jail right now, so I flew up here to get away."

"Look man, that don't sound like Ania, hell no."

"I know but females get weak."

"Yeah, yeah, you gotta point there. I definitely know about that. Been on both sides of that shit." Isaiah thinks for a minute. "So, what's your plan?"

"Got to leave her, if and once she comes clean, and if it takes her too long to admit, I'm just gonna raise up. I been thinking, we had a good run. We raised a hell of a son.

Maybe it's time. I don't even want to discuss the other alternative 'cause it's going to put me behind bars, and a man only does what a woman lets him in the first place."

"Check this out. Worst case scenario. If she did it, you don't think you can take her back? It happens all the time. It will be work involved, that kind of pain ain't no joke. But you can't throw away good years like that bruh."

Larenz doesn't give it any thought. "No way, if something like that happened it makes you wonder if those years were that good in the first place. Look, I'm going back tomorrow and if things are as they appear, it's over."

Larenz and Isaiah continue to hang out during the day, hitting Gibson's for a great steak, then over to Biggs Mansion to pick up a couple of $300 sticks. Then they go to a lounge to smoke them and drink some yac. It is hard for Isaiah to gage what Larenz is planning to do even though he'd already told him. But Isaiah, doesn't want to hear it, he knows how full of it Bill is and when they were growing up couldn't stand his backstabbing ass. Every time he would hear something about Bill he would believe it because that's how he rolls. Isaiah doesn't want Ania and Larenz to end things because deep down inside he knows there is not one other woman in the world that will love him like she does.

–

The next morning over breakfast, Isaiah's words go unheard by Larenz after hearing all the reasons Isaiah believes he is moving too quickly in his decision-making process and destroying a rock strong relationship. To no avail, in Larenz's view of things, there is nothing Isaiah can say to him that will make him change his conviction. He's made up his mind. He's going back home to get the truth once and for all and bids Isaiah farewell.

–

Larenz steps into first class on the plane ready to get back home. When he looks up, someone is in his seat and trying to get themselves situated, then turns around.

"I like the window black man, take the aisle," Isaiah tells him.

"Bruh, what, what's going on?"

"You know I can't let you go back home like this. We're going to handle this shit. You better believe that." Isaiah, puts out his fist and they pound up.

Larenz says, "Yeah, you're right." He pulls out his phone. "Let me sit my ass down, at least let Ania know I'm okay. I gotta be grown about this."

Isaiah says, "Just sit back and think about your future, I called her yesterday."

"You did?"

"Yeah, I think I interrupted a prayer meeting or something. I think they was praying over your black ass."

They fist bump again and ask the stewardess for a bottle and they don't care how early in the morning it is.

–

Before they take off, Larenz texts JT to pick him up at the airport; JT is right there to scoop him and Isaiah up. JT gets out his ride as soon as he sees Larenz walk out of the airport. He walks over to him. "Bruh, I should whoop your gatdamn ass," JT tells him. He grabs then hugs his boy and pushes him a bit letting him know he wants to rough him up; all Larenz can do is smile.

Isaiah daps up JT and says, "How do you think I felt when I saw him back in the city? This guy…."

JT says, "Everybody you know been lookin' for you. Do you know I almost killed Bill over the fact he came in the club talking nonsense."

Larenz says, "Oh yeah?"

"Hell, yeah, but he's not a problem anymore; our business with him is over, all he needs to do is drop off the check and move the hell on."

"When is he supposed to do that?" Larenz wants to know.

"Around three at the club."

Isaiah looks up from texting on his phone. "Yo, let me handle that for you? Let me take the meet. I think it's time I had a little chat with ya mans."

"Yeah, that would be a good time for me to talk to Ania anyway."

"Ah, ah ah, your girl said she doesn't want to see you until tomorrow," Isaiah says.

"Tomorrow?"

"That's what she told me on the phone."

"Probably going to get her hair done and get all fine for you bruh. You know how they like to do it," JT says.

Larenz thinks about it. "Well, I don't care how fine she looks, all I have is one question and then we will see."

—

Three o'clock rolls around, and JT takes Larenz over to see the work on the commercial property, and Isaiah is at the club sitting behind Larenz's desk, waiting for Bill to show up. Calvin brings him back, then leaves them to it.

"Isaiah, is that you?" Bill says.

"Yeah, it's me, brother. It's me."

Bill looks around surprised. "My man, good to see you." He attempts to shake hands with Isaiah but Isaiah doesn't budge.

"Larenz asked me to tell you to put his check on the desk."

"Okay, what's the tone about bruh, damn?"

"You already know, I'm down here on the insanity going on."

"Oh, that craziness that happened the other night? Bruh, I'm past that, moving on, you know what I'm saying? I have come down to Atlanta and did what I needed to do, and I'm out. Kind of tired of this dusty muthafuka anyway."

Isaiah says, "Good, then you can stop these games you're playing, man, and my good people can continue with their good life."

Bill says, "I don't know what you're talking about?"

Isaiah shakes his finger at Bill in remembrance. "You know, when we were younger, I use to think you was just one of the dumbest negroes that I ever ran across in my life. But as we have grown older, I know for a gotdamn fact, you are. You're out here getting in-between what two friends have built up over the years."

"Nah, I was here on love, I put money in his pockets."

"Your money doesn't mean anything, and what you're doing business wise don't mean a damn thing either. Larenz does-not-need-your-money. He is a true and tried, battle tested business man. As a matter of fact, the music you've been letting these piss-ass acts of yours put out over the years hasn't done nothing but set our people back damn near a hundred years."

Bill says, "In your eyes. Get outta here with that–sh…"

"Look, stop running your mouth about Ania, and more importantly, stop lying on her."

Bill looks at Isaiah strong. "Or what?"

"You don't want to find out," Isaiah lets him know.

"Look, you don't know who you're talking to Isaiah so stay in your slow little lane you've carved out for yourself."

"Oh, it's like that?"

Bill goes into his suit jacket, grabs the check, and places it on the desk; he taps it with his forefinger a few times. "Just like that. Give that to your boy for me." Then he turns and walks away.

Shook

Because the facility is good with letting Nicole go back home, Ania, Jill, and Lisa leave in the morning to pick her up and wouldn't be back at the house until somewhere around one-o'clock.

JT is driving with Larenz and Isaiah to take Larenz home and says, "It's going to be okay bruh. I have all the faith in you two. Ain't no way, things are going to go down other than a positive outcome. And that's on GOD."

Isaiah looks up from his phone in the back. "Amen, Amen."

Larenz says, "Well, we will see. All I want to know is one answer, ya dig."

JT pulls into the driveway, "Well, here we are."

Larenz looks outside his house and sees Ania, Nicole, Lisa, Jill, Jacob, Zoe and Kerry waiting for him. Nicole is sitting in a wheelchair; the doctors said she needs to stay off her feet for a week because she twisted her ankle running from the police.

Larenz looks around at everyone, then towards Isaiah and JT. "What's all this?"

Isaiah says, "Restoration and peace. Restoration and peace my brother."

JT turns off the car and they all get out. Everyone walks over to Larenz and gives him hugs and much love. Jacob embraces his pops and then wipes his tears away when he lets him go. Soon after, Ania walks up to him and grabs his hand. They walk away a few steps where they can be alone, get some privacy as everyone else chit-chats, and are happy as can be, Larenz is home.

Larenz looks around and says, "Hey, uhh, do you know Lisa is standing in our front yard?"

Ania smiles. "Yes, I know."

He says, "What, what's going on?"

"We straightened all that mess out. I truly get where she was coming from with her poem and all. Look, sometimes all you gotta do is talk it out."

Larenz looks at Ania and then Lisa again. "Okay…."

She says, "Look baby you are all that I want. You are all that I will ever want, and I need you to believe that."

"But Ania, … I need to."

"No, just listen. I need you in my life and there is no way

you're ever going to leave me."

"Yeah, all that is good, but I need to know something, and I need to know the truth."

Right then and there, they hear Nicole scream, "Here his ass comes y'all! Ania, here he comes!" Everyone has their eyes on the car rolling up and stopping in front of the house and Bill gets out. Larenz sees him and starts to walk over, but JT grabs him by the arm.

JT says, "Bruh, that's the same car I saw."

Larenz tries again to walk over to Bill, but Isaiah grabs him. "Hold on, hold on."

Bill is standing looking at the gathering.

Nicole has a very sarcastic tone and sings, "Hey….. Bill…" He smiles at the same time; trying to figure out what's going on. "Hey Nicole you doing alright?"

Nicole says, "Yeah, I'm good, since I realized you ain't shit." He looks around when he hears some laughs, gasps.

Bill says, "Say what?"

Nicole says, "Don't say what me; like you don't know. Out here trying to upset my mental."

Bill squints his eyes and places a look of slight embarrassment on his face. "What, what're you talking about?"

"You know exactly what I'm talking about. Us getting married and living your rich lifestyle all that noise you been talking to me for years just feeding me your lies."

Bill smiles from embarrassment. "Now c'mon you know I never meant any of that. Look at you."

"No nigga, look at you. You sorry ass bastard."

Jill and Kerry pull out some papers. "And stop sending us contracts to your lame ass label," Jill says.

"Already told you not interested," Kerry lets him know, then they rip them up and throw the pieces in his direction.

Isaiah points and nods his head. "Now, look down the street, here comes somebody you know with your punk ass."

A car with a driver pulls up, stops and a woman gets out the car and those who know her call out her name.

Bill says, "Sheila, what're you doing here?"

She says, "What do you mean, what am I doing here? I'm your wife."

Everyone is shocked and repeats her words.

Isaiah says, "See, I told you don't try me, didn't I?"

Sheila says, "Do you think that square ass cruise and waiting on you in Monaco was going to keep me from finding out about all the mess you keep going on? Isaiah has had my back all these years and you didn't even know it."

Isaiah mumbles, "That's right beloved, I done had more than that."

Jill sings, "Hey…."

Sheila walks over to everyone, greets them, then stops at Larenz. "Look at you Larenz, still fine as you want to be. First, let me apologize for that sorry excuse of a man standing over there. And let me tell you something. I know first-hand that he did not sleep with Ania."

"Oh, really," Larenz says.

"That's right because he told me so, when we all lived in Chicago. He came to me upset that she wouldn't because she was so in love with you. Plus, I told him if he had, I wouldn't go out with him myself because it would have been reckless 'cause that's not how friends do. So, no, he didn't; so, all you need to do is keep loving on your wife like you have been doing all these years and forget all the foolish mess he's been saying."

Bill is standing looking like a complete simpleton.

Sheila says as she looks at Bill, "I'm sorry I even married this sorry ass want-to-be-playboy, and I'm especially sorry to you, Nicole when this fool is throwing all that nonsense to you talking about he wants to get married. I'm completely embarrassed."

Nicole smiles, "It's okay, you can have him sis."

Sheila says, "Well, I don't want him."

Bill turns his head to her quick, "What? Then he looks over at the car when the window is rolled down on his side. "And who is that in the car with you?"

She tells him, "My lawyer, and after you sign these divorce papers, he'll be the man I'll be freakin' until I'm tired, you got that? So, get ready to sign, or I'll have your ass on TTMZ so fast your pin-head ass will spin. Sheila looks at a for sale sign right across the street. "Ania and Larenz, I think as soon as the ink dries on those divorce papers, I'm buying that house across the street, and we're gonna be neighbors, so we can kick it like we used to and make fun of Bill's deceitful ass." Bill is shaken to no end. "Now c'mon Bill, go sign the papers and while you're doing that, I'm going to see if I can get a tour of my new house." Sheila takes off walking. "C'mon with your lying ass."

Bill starts to follow Sheila and looks back, "Y'all ain't

shit."

Nicole waves from her chair. "Bye, little dick. So glad we didn't get married. I could tell you couldn't do the nasty. And to think he thought he was gonna get a piece of this. Please, I may be crazy, but I ain't stupid."

Larenz grabs Ania by the hand and kisses her, and JT walks over. JT says, "My bad bruh, but I did see him creeping. But I guess he was going to the back to see Nicole."

Ania says, "Guess, my ass, he did go to the back to see her." They laugh.

JT says, "My bad, but this is my boy."

Ania points to JT and smiles. "Mind your business JT, mind your business." Ania kisses Larenz. "It's okay, I'm forgetting all about this and letting you make it up to me."

Larenz grabs her by the waist. "Really? You will let me do that?"

She says, "Umm…hmm all night long and then we're going on a vacation."

He says, "Bet, let's do it."

The sun is shining bright, and everyone is gathered around in Larenz and Ania Ways front yard, joking about the look on Bill's long face while marching to the car with the lawyer, to sign his divorce papers. Sheila struts across the street in her sundress and sandals to view the house for sale, all the while mentioning Bill's nonsense out loud. JT extends his hand to Lisa and introduces himself all over again. She smiles and so does he.

Music by Franklin White related to **Ways of Love available at** Franklin-White.com

www.ingramcontent.com/pod-product-compliance
Lightning Source LLC
Chambersburg PA
CBHW030811310726
48980CB00006B/454/J